Emmy was afraid to breathe in case the fantasy ended.

Sam was kissing her, and definitely not in any chaste fashion that could be open to misinterpretation.

Why should she care what had prompted him to make a move tonight if it was making all of her wildest dreams come true? She would be remiss not to enjoy everything he was offering. This could be her only chance. She had skipped to the head of the queue, and rather than feel guilty about those she might have pushed past, she decided to party the rest of the night away.

"Do you want to come back to my room?"

"You're sure about this?" Sam was giving her another chance to back out if she wanted. One look at him, so handsome in his suit, with the moonlight highlighting the sparkle in his eyes and that sexy dimple in his cheek, and she had never been more sure of anything in her life. For one night only Sam was going to be hers, and she was not going to miss another minute of it.

Dear Reader,

Most of us have insecurities about our appearance but for Emmy Jennings, these hang-ups are only intensified by her family circumstances. Having been adopted by a family who went on to have beautiful identical twin girls left her feeling unwanted as well as inadequate.

It's only natural she's been harboring a crush for years on her brother's best friend, Sam Goodwin, who accepts her for exactly who she is—something a lot of people would love to have in a prospective partner!

A night of passion and a pregnancy later, it's Sam who proposes the idea of getting married to give Emmy and the baby some security. A marriage that turns out to be anything other than convenient when they're fighting against their feelings for one another…

I hope you enjoy Emmy and Sam's journey to find themselves as well as one another. The course of true love never runs smoothly but hopefully it's all worth it in the end.

Happy reading!

Lots of love,

Karin x

WED FOR THEIR ONE NIGHT BABY

———

KARIN BAINE

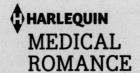

HARLEQUIN

MEDICAL
ROMANCE

HARLEQUIN®
MEDICAL
ROMANCE™

Recycling programs
for this product may
not exist in your area.

ISBN-13: 978-1-335-40909-6

Wed for Their One Night Baby

Copyright © 2022 by Karin Baine

All rights reserved. No part of this book may be used or reproduced in
any manner whatsoever without written permission except in the case of
brief quotations embodied in critical articles and reviews.

This is a work of fiction. Names, characters, places and incidents
are either the product of the author's imagination or are used fictitiously.
Any resemblance to actual persons, living or dead, businesses,
companies, events or locales is entirely coincidental.

This edition published by arrangement with Harlequin Books S.A.

For questions and comments about the quality of this book,
please contact us at CustomerService@Harlequin.com.

Harlequin Enterprises ULC
22 Adelaide St. West, 41st Floor
Toronto, Ontario M5H 4E3, Canada
www.Harlequin.com

Printed in U.S.A.

Karin Baine lives in Northern Ireland with her husband, two sons and her out-of-control notebook collection. Her mother and her grandmother's vast collection of books inspired her love of reading and her dream of becoming a Harlequin author. Now she can tell people she has a *proper* job! You can follow Karin on Twitter, @karinbaine1, or visit her website for the latest news—karinbaine.com.

Books by Karin Baine

Harlequin Medical Romance

Pups that Make Miracles
Their One-Night Christmas Gift

Single Dad Docs
The Single Dad's Proposal

Paddington Children's Hospital
Falling for the Foster Mom

Midwife Under the Mistletoe
Their One-Night Twin Surprise
Healed by Their Unexpected Family
Reunion with His Surgeon Princess
One Night with Her Italian Doc
The Surgeon and the Princess
The Nurse's Christmas Hero

Visit the Author Profile page
at Harlequin.com for more titles.

For my Maisie Moo xx

CHAPTER ONE

ONE OF THESE girls is not like the others...
The words sing-songed in Emmy's head as
the wedding guests focused on her and her
sisters, Lorna and Lisa, at the top table. She
knew they were studying the three of them
and seeing the physical differences.

The need to deflect their stares was as necessary to her as breathing. A defence mecha-
nism developed from childhood to pre-empt
any insults thrown her way, having received
many over the years. She had never seemed
to fit in anywhere. A legacy of being bounced
around the care system at a young age, she
supposed. Given up by her parents at the tender age of three and moved between foster
homes until she was adopted at five, she remembered too much of it.

It was difficult enough being big sister
to identical twins who were not related to

her by blood, but she could not have looked more different. They were slim with porcelain skin and long blond hair. She was curvy, with caramel-coloured skin and dark corkscrew curls. A product of a mixed-race partnership, which she unfortunately knew nothing about because she had not had any contact with her birth parents since they had given her up. Thankfully, the Jennings family had adopted her, and she was lucky enough to have David as her big brother who treated her just the same as his two biological sisters. Unfortunately, it also meant being part of the bridal party on display today.

'I've known Dave for pretty much my whole life and, Bryony, you couldn't ask for a better husband.' Sam Goodwin's best man's speech drew a chorus of 'Aws,' along with Emmy's attention. Not only had he been sincere and funny in all the right places, but he looked damn hot in his grey, silk morning suit, and baby pink cravat.

Emmy had harboured a crush on her brother's best friend for as long as she could remember. Even when he had not looked this hot. During their teenage years he would frequently turn up on their doorstep splattered with mud, holding a football under his arm, looking for his mate. To her dismay he had treated her like his little sister too. Someone to tease, someone to confide in when needed and someone he looked out for. Unfortunately, that also meant Emmy being rendered invisible where Sam's love life was concerned.

Nothing romantic had ever happened between them but with a never-ending supply of new girlfriends, he never had reason to look at the chubby, frizzy-haired kid with a crush on him. Emmy wondered who was lined up tonight to occupy his bed as he had not brought a plus one with him to the reception.

'I want to take this chance to say thanks to the beautiful bridesmaids who've been taking excellent care of the bride today. To the beautiful bridesmaids,' he said, lifting his glass to encourage the rest of the guests to repeat the toast. Emmy shifted uncomfortably in her seat as all eyes were directed towards her again.

'Hey! Don't forget about me too,' she shouted from the far end of the table, raising the laughs she was aiming for. Except from Sam, who was trying to burn a hole through her with a pointed look. Clearly unamused by the interruption. Too bad. It was his own fault. He should know her well enough to expect her to open her big gob and spoil the moment when she was under pressure.

She stuck her tongue out at him in another fit of pique, so he would get back to the job at hand. Which he did.

'Anyway, we all wish you good health and happiness, Dave and Bryony.' He lifted his glass again. 'To the bride and groom.'

This time Emmy was happy to join in with the toast. However, she did not miss Sam's glance at her or the shake of his head.

'What?' she mouthed in response and shrugged, feigning innocence.

At least now the dinner and speeches were over Emmy could climb down off this stage and fade back into the crowd. Bryony had likely only included her in the bridal party to save her from sitting on her own. Honestly, she could have done without the spotlight. Not to mention the humiliation of the dresses when she was at least double the size of the other bridesmaids. The strapless pink silk ensembles hugged her sisters' slim bodies beautifully, but Emmy had spent the entire day hoisting hers up, trying to avoid flashing her bountiful assets at the congregation.

The wedding pictures had been mortifying, getting shifted around until the photographer had given up trying to hide her curves between the willowy blondes. As usual, she looked completely out of place next to them.

The chunky five-year-old the Jenningses had taken in had not really changed. For the first few years of her new life, she had had her big brother to adore. Just the two of them playing and sharing adventures and bonding together. Then the miracle twins had been born. The biological baby girls her adoptive parents thought they were too old to conceive.

With their hands full looking after two babies, they had left a lot of Emmy-sitting to David, though he was still a child himself. She was no longer the youngest and Emmy supposed it was around that time she had become the joker in the family. Fooling around for laughs and attention from their parents, believing she had become the unwanted houseguest once the twins arrived. The treats and special outings she had revelled in as the latest addition to the Jennings clan had promptly stopped until she felt like more of a nuisance. As though looking after an adopted mixed-race child was more hassle on top of twin babies.

Still, the Jenningses were her family. The only ones willing to put up with her. Her birth parents had not been so inclined…

'Why did you do that?' The sound of Sam's voice startled her into almost spilling her champagne.

The hotel staff were clearing the tables away to get ready for the evening celebrations and Emmy had taken herself to the bar to avoid any more photographs or attention. She was not in the mood to socialise.

'Why did I do what?' she asked, leaning back against the bar. The best way to survive this night was probably to drink enough to forget she was here on her own and not care what people thought about her. As if there was sufficient alcohol in the world to do that. Constantly worrying about being liked and accepted was the permanent hangover she carried from her unstable early years.

Sam ordered himself a whisky before he answered. He was standing so close to her, that woody aftershave of his was doing strange things to her insides. The scent alone an aphrodisiac she did not need when she was probably the only single thirty-something here. Apart from Sam, who had never looked twice at her.

With his gaze fixed on the bartender, Emmy took the opportunity to study him up close. It had been a while since she had last seen him. They only met at these occasional family get-togethers which he was always invited to, but where he was usually occupied with his female companion of the moment. He had clearly made an effort with his appearance for the occasion. Not that he had to work too hard to get female attention. His usually mussed dark brown hair had been clipped short and the scruff of beard around his full lips shorn away. He looked like the boy next door, except with sexy come-to-bed grey-blue eyes and pretty, long dark lashes. More like the naughty neighbour who would pop round for a roll in bed when your parents were out.

Nope. She still was not over her childhood crush.

'Why did you put yourself down like that?' he asked, tossing back the golden liquor handed over to him. A grimace, then he slammed the empty glass back on the counter. Apparently the responsibility of his role today had been stressful for him too.

'Sorry if I ruined your deeply heartfelt platitudes.' Emmy washed her sarcasm down with a sip of champagne, the bubbles tickling her throat on the way down. Adding to that fizzing sensation already going on inside her.

Sam gave her his trademark half-smile that perfectly displayed the deep dimple in his cheek. 'You know that's not what I'm talking about.'

'No? I thought you were mad at me for interrupting your sensitive best friend act. I assumed you were advertising for a wedding night sex buddy since you came unattached today.' She was attempting the sassy banter she was known for but there was jealousy at play behind the teasing. Sam appeared to have hooked up with every woman who had ever crossed his path. Except her. It was only natural she should wonder what was wrong with her when it was a question she had been asking herself her whole life.

What was wrong with her that her birth parents gave her away after three years of raising her? That her adoptive parents wanted more children even after taking her on? Why didn't her ex-boyfriends see her as a long-term prospect?

'Ouch!' With a hand clutching his chest, Sam staggered backwards. 'So cynical.'

'Uh-huh. I know you, remember? So, who have you got your eye on?' She glanced around the room. 'Is it the redhead wearing the scrap of ice-blue lace or...the mother of the bride? Do you go for the sexy older woman? Do you even have a type?' Whatever it was, it clearly was not her.

'Believe it or not, Emmy-Lou, I am here for your brother's sake, not my libido.'

She raised an eyebrow, waiting for the punchline.

'Besides, if I brought a woman to a wedding, she might get romantic notions I have no intention of being party to.' Sam caught the attention of the barman and shook his empty glass.

'What is your aversion to commitment, Sam Goodwin? One of these days your looks will fade, and you'll be forced to rely on your personality alone to hook women. I'm not sure that's gonna cut it. You could end up a sad, lonely man.' She sucked a breath in through her teeth, not believing it any more than he would. There had been a steady queue of women waiting for his attention since they were teenagers.

Emmy was not even in the queue. Merely on the sidelines watching as he made his way along it.

'I'm married to the job. You know that.' It was true, he was a dedicated consultant paediatrician, popular with staff and patients alike by all accounts. However, she was sure Sam's father being absent for most of his childhood had something to do with his inability to settle down. Sam had spent a lot of time over at the Jennings house and seemed to live independently from his family at a young age. Emmy supposed he had got too used to it.

'Anyway, you can talk, Emmy-Lou Jennings. Shouldn't you be married with a load of kids by now? Your sisters seem keen to get those rings on their fingers.' He nodded towards the twins and their appropriately handsome, financially stable boyfriends. At least they were taken. If Sam had designs on either of them, she did not think she would have made it through the night without breaking down.

'It's not for want of trying,' she muttered, thankful that Sam was too busy getting a whisky refill to hear her. She sounded pathetic. Desperate. She had never managed to hold down a long-term relationship but not through choice. When she had brought up the subject of a future with her last boyfriend, he had literally laughed in her face.

'No offence, Em, but I'm with you for a good time, not a long time.'

Who would not have taken offence at that? Worse than that, most of her exes had gone on to marry and have children so it was not the idea of settling down they had an issue with, just the idea of doing it with her. She was still getting passed around like an unwanted gift, never finding the right fit. Apparently she was okay to sleep with but not wife material. Whatever that was. Not that she was in any rush to get down the aisle whatever the cost, but it would be nice to have someone in her life she could see herself having a future with. Despite her troubled upbringing, or perhaps because of it, she wanted babies of her own. A family she truly belonged to.

'Maybe I'm married to my job too.' It was an attempt to deflect the sad truth of her love life. As a paediatric nurse she worked equally unsociable hours and could therefore use it as an excuse for still living on her own just as he had.

Sam raised his glass in a toast. 'To the job.'

Emmy clinked what was left of her champagne to it.

'You still haven't answered my question though, Emmy-Lou.'

'Emmy. I don't know why you insist on using that name. It makes me sound eight years old.' Emma-Louise was her given name, but David had always shortened it to Emmy-Lou to tease her. When Sam called her that, it made her feel like his kid sister. No woman wanted that from the man she had had a life-long crush on.

'Stop trying to change the subject, *Emmy*. Why did you make that joke? You're always putting yourself down in front of others.' He spoke as though she was someone to be pitied, making her defences spring up twice as fast.

'Cheap laughs? Your speech was getting

kinda soppy and I thought it needed lightening up.'

'You don't fool me. We practically grew up together and I know you always make yourself the butt of your own jokes.'

'Well, it is quite a butt.' She fluttered her eyelashes and patted her ample behind to a roll of Sam's grey-blue eyes.

'Just stop it,' he said, so forcefully and with such authority that Emmy immediately stopped fooling around.

'I only say what everyone else is thinking. It's not an insult if I get in there first.' It was unnerving that he had seen right through her jolly façade to the imposter child who was on the verge of tears at being found out.

'There's no need for it,' he said, much softer now. 'Just because you look different to your sisters, it doesn't make you any less beautiful.'

He reached out and let his fingers brush against her cheek.

Emmy momentarily stopped breathing. Was Sam actually showing an interest in her beyond their usual back and forth banter?

There was no time to analyse what was happening or how intensely Sam was looking at her as the DJ announced the first dance.

'We should, uh, probably go and…' Uncharacteristically flustered by the interaction, Emmy struggled to find any coherent words. The idea that her long-term unrequited love might actually be reciprocated had totally thrown her off form.

'Yes. I suppose we should.' After setting their glasses down, Sam took her hand and led her towards the dance floor.

In all the years she had known Sam he had never once flirted with her, not even in jest. Perhaps now they were both grown up she was considered fair game and they did not come much gamer than her tonight.

Everyone applauded the newlyweds as they twirled around the floor, wrapped up in each other and the beauty of the moment. Emmy had to swallow the ache of emotion welling in her throat to see her big brother so happy. She had always been grateful to David for accepting her as family even when his real sisters came along and loved him unconditionally. To see him smiling as though he had won life's lottery made her truly happy for him.

'Can we have the rest of the bridal party on the floor, please?' the DJ requested, with David and Bryony beckoning to them.

'Looks like we're up,' Sam said, leading Emmy out to meet them. He slid his hands around her waist, Emmy circled her arms around his neck and they swayed together to the slow beat. Oblivious to the crowd watching, or the other couples who joined them. Her inner teenager's heart was full to bursting as Sam held her close.

'This is a first,' she said with a nervous giggle. 'I don't think we've ever danced together.'

'There are a whole lot of things we've never done together.' Sam's voice was low in her ear, full of innuendo and promise. Emmy had no idea what had brought about this sudden change in their usually platonic relationship, but she was enjoying it. It was the perfect balm to soothe the rawness of her recent break-up. To know she might be wanted and by someone she had fancied ever since those first teenage hormones had kicked in.

'Are you coming on to me, Mr Goodwin?' She clutched at the gold 'Bridesmaid' necklace Bryony had presented her with this morning, in fake horror.

Sam chuckled. 'Would that be such a terrible idea?'

'Probably.' The confirmation made her a tad breathless.

'We've always enjoyed one another's company and we're both single…'

'Why now?' Despite the euphoria there was a niggle of doubt refusing to let her get too carried away by the idea he wanted her.

'I don't know. Right time, right place, and I have a feeling you and I would have a really good time together. On our own.'

Emmy's good mood deflated as quickly as a burst balloon. She dropped her arms from around his neck. 'I see. I'm convenient. You won't have to work too hard with me.'

Tears were burning the backs of her eyes as she refused to let them fall. Sam was just another man who saw her as a good-time girl. Someone to kill time with until a better prospect came along. It hurt more from him because he had known her for most of her life. She guessed that did not mean as much to him as it did to her when he was willing to forget their shared past for the sake of a quick hook-up.

'I think you have the wrong girl,' she said quietly before fleeing the room just as the song ended.

* * *

Sam could only watch helplessly as Emmy took off. He did not want to cause a scene and draw attention by calling her or running after her when all eyes were still on the bride and groom. A round of applause accompanied the couple as they left the floor and came to join him.

'Where did Emmy disappear to?' Dave asked on his way towards the bar.

'I, er, think she got a bit emotional. Needed some fresh air.' Sam had played it completely wrong with her and stuffed everything up. Emmy had looked so beautiful tonight he could not stop himself from flirting with her. Forgetting she was not someone he could simply walk away from the next day. Not that he would have wanted to, he was sure. He had always had a soft spot for her when she was so easy to talk to. Unlike the spoiled, superficial girls who had chased after him in high school, only interested in being popular and showing off. Emmy was thoughtful, funny and adorable. Unfortunately, she was also his best friend's little sister and Dave would have pulverised him if he had ever made a move on her. He still might.

Perhaps it was the shot of Scottish courage or seeing her again for the first in a long time that had made him act so recklessly. More than likely it was actually having her in his arms, holding her so close, that had prompted his proposition. Usually the rest of the Jennings clan were in attendance, preventing any private time, but tonight they were all otherwise engaged.

'Can I get you a drink?' Dave slapped him on the back.

'I'm fine, thanks. I should be the one buying drinks to celebrate you being a married man.'

'Don't worry, Bryony's dad is paying,' he said, ordering a bottle of lager.

A few more guests appeared to offer their congratulations, and once Dave's attention was diverted elsewhere, Sam took the opportunity to slip away. He needed to find Emmy and apologise for being so crass. She was more sensitive than she pretended to be and he of all people should have remembered that.

When he had frequently used the Jennings house as an escape, Emmy used to join him and Dave to play board games, cards or listen to music. Sometimes, if Dave was out or busy with something else, he and Emmy would have hung out together anyway. As angst-ridden teens they used to confide in each other. Emmy had had her problems with bullying and being made to feel like an outcast, while he had to deal with his father's frequent absences and the difficulties that left at home. Finding that common ground with someone who understood there were more important issues than having the latest fads or not wearing the right clothes let Sam know he was not alone in the world. It made things a little easier when he had someone who understood life on a deeper emotional level to talk to.

On the outside no one would have known he or Emmy was struggling. She played the clown, often making jokes at her own expense, trying to make friends with everyone. Sam used to put on a façade the same way she did. His reputation as a ladies' man might have been deserved but it hid what was really going on inside him. Having a string of girlfriends was an attempt to make him feel good, so he was never on his own. The way he had often felt with his father gone and his mother pushing him away because he reminded her too much of her two-timing husband.

Anyone who entered into a relationship with Sam knew from the outset he would not commit to anything long term.

The truth was he was afraid of causing anyone the same pain his father had inflicted on him and his mother. At least Sam was honest in telling prospective partners he would not be there for them. Unlike his dad, who had constantly disappointed and hurt the ones he was supposed to love.

Sam knew all that self-deprecating humour of Emmy's was a flimsy cover to protect her soft heart. He had simply forgotten in a moment of lust-filled weakness and now he had to make amends or his conscience would plague him for ever.

The lobby of the hotel was filled with guests chatting and drinking but there was no sign of Emmy among them. She tended to stand out in a room because of her huge personality and warmth which drew people towards her. Yet, with a few misjudged words, he had made her disappear. The last thing he had wanted to do was upset Emmy when he had been so looking forward to seeing her again.

She had always seemed to understand him the way no one else ever had. Perhaps because they both had that same sense of abandonment by their parents and were grateful to the Jennings family for welcoming them in. Unlike the younger members of the Jennings siblings, Emmy had made him feel comfortable there. Of course, he and Dave were close, but his best mate would never understand the worry and fear of not belonging or being loved, the way Emmy did.

He had parents who doted on him. Not a father who used to disappear for months on end leaving his family to fend for themselves. Emmy could relate to that kind of loneliness, but it was not always easy to get her on her own to talk to. It became harder once they had all grown up, moved on to college and gone their separate ways. Only meeting up on occasions such as this. Now he had upset her he might never get to see her again. The thought was too depressing to contemplate. He had to make things right.

Sam headed outside. It was dark now, with a nip in the air. Only the hardiest smokers appeared to have ventured beyond the warmth of the hotel, huddled at the main entrance in a cloud of smoke.

Sam squeezed past and walked away from the giddy guests, sure Emmy would have sought privacy elsewhere. There were plenty of places to hide across the vast country estate now that the night was closing in.

He followed the path away from the hotel, past the gazebo and gardens where the wedding photographs were taken earlier. Even then Emmy had joked that it would look like she had eaten the other bridesmaids if she was forced to stand up front and insisted on hiding away at the back of the group. The twins had happily shown off for the cameras while he and Emmy had messed around in the background, pouting like ducks and generally acting the idiots. Having fun together to hide the embarrassment of being in the spotlight. It had felt like old times, when he had escaped to the Jennings house because things were rocky at home. Emmy had always been there with a laugh and a joke to make things better or a listening ear when he needed one. Spending today with her was what he had needed after another stressful break-up.

Despite being honest with Caroline that he did not want anything serious, she had tried to force him into a 'proper' relationship. Her constant hints about moving in together or wanting to introduce him to her parents had signalled the end for Sam. They had not been together long, but telling her he did not want to see her any more had brought more tears and anger from Caroline than he had expected. Apparently dating any woman over thirty was leading her on if he had no intention of getting married or having babies. Dating at his age was beginning to get messy.

Perhaps that was why he had propositioned Emmy tonight. She had reminded him of the old days, when they had been able to be themselves with one another without things getting complicated. The time they had spent together today larking about had revived those old feelings he had had for her, and he had acted on them this time without thinking about the consequences.

Sam spotted a figure down by the river sitting on the white wrought-iron swing seat and instantly knew it was her.

'Emmy? I'm so sorry for upsetting you,' he said quietly as he approached her.

'It's okay.' She did not look at him, continuing to rock the seat back and forward.

He hopped on beside her, took her chin between his thumb and forefinger and forced her to look at him. Seeing her tears glistening in the moonlight almost broke his heart knowing he had caused them.

'I was an insensitive prat.'

'Yes, you were, but what's new?' Emmy stuck her tongue out in her usual playful fashion but the tear running down her cheek belied her real feelings.

Sam caught it on the back of his finger and wiped it away, wishing he could erase the hurt he had caused her so easily.

'I really am sorry. I wouldn't hurt you for the world, Emmy.'

'It's fine. I'm a big girl. I have a hide like a rhinoceros.'

He put his finger to her lips before she could say anything else derogatory about herself.

'Shh!' He was all too aware of her soft full lips against his finger and it was easy to let his mind wander about what it would be like to kiss them. Not for the first time.

Emmy was watching him with those big

brown eyes and waiting for him to let her speak. Except he did not want the talking to ruin things again. Instead, he did what he had wanted to do for as long as he could remember and leaned in. Gently replacing his finger with his readied lips, to taste her, to marry his mouth to hers and express everything she meant to him in a passionate kiss.

Emmy was afraid to breathe in case the fantasy ended. Sam was kissing her and definitely not in any chaste fashion which could be open to misinterpretation. It was blowing her mind to find he might actually be romantically interested in her. The way she had always thought of him. Yet here he was, cupping her face in his hands, kissing her slowly and gently teasing her tongue with his.

Everything in her wanted to believe him when he said this was not a matter of convenience. That he wanted her, only her, in this moment. It was not as though she was expecting him to declare his undying devotion to her and get down on one knee to propose. Was it? Perhaps in her more whimsical fantasies, where they married and lived happily ever after with their chubby little babies.

In reality, all she wanted was for Sam to notice her the way he noticed every other woman. Let her believe for a while that she was not completely hideous. She had dreamed of his touch, this kiss, and it seemed as though the next logical step was to let nature take its course. Why deny herself the pleasure of Sam Goodwin and let paranoia win?

Why should she care what had prompted him to make a move tonight if it was making all of her wildest dreams come true? She would be crazy not to enjoy everything he was offering. This could be her only chance. Next time she saw him he was sure to have hooked up with a new leggy beauty. This was her time. She had skipped to the head of the queue and, rather than feel guilty about those she might have pushed past, she decided to party the rest of the night away.

'Do you want to come back to my room?' It was a bold move from someone who had been sobbing only moments ago because no one wanted to be with her for any meaningful kind of relationship. Now Emmy was willing to put the one she did have with Sam on the line for the sake of one night in his bed.

Exactly the type of move he probably made

on a regular basis without his conscience bothering him. Emmy decided it was just what she needed after being dumped again. Rebound sex with someone who was well versed in one-night-stand etiquette would give her confidence a much-needed boost.

'Don't you think we'll be missed?' It was not a 'no,' making Emmy all the more determined to see this through.

'Not for a while. We can always come back down later.' Doing things this way could make it less awkward than having to face each other in the morning. There would be no confusion about what this was. A hookup. Not even a full night together. No reason for either of them to stress over it at a later date. They were two consenting, single adults looking for a little company.

'You're sure about this?' Sam was giving her another chance to back out if she wanted. One look at him, so handsome in his suit, with the moonlight highlighting the sparkle in his eyes and that sexy dimple in his cheek, and she had never been more sure of anything in her life. For one night only, Sam was going to be hers and she was not going to miss another minute of it.

Even the thought of finally sharing a bed with him made her shiver. Goosebumps popped over her skin as she anticipated his touch.

'I'm sure.'

'Let's get you somewhere warm.' He shrugged off his jacket and draped it around her shoulders as he led her back towards the hotel.

She practically floated back to her room, half convinced she must be dreaming. Until they were alone in her room and the air between them was sparking with sexual awareness.

After this, there would be no going back. They could never look at each other the same way again. A shame when this shared, hungry-for-one-another exchange was so hot.

Instead, they proceeded, wordless and breathless, to take off one another's clothes. This was the point when Emmy usually insisted on turning out the light, sucking in her tummy and trying her best to be someone else in the dark. Here, with Sam, she did not need to do any of that. He knew exactly who he was dealing with and what he was getting. Besides, she had fantasised about this moment long enough that she wished to see Sam in all of his splendour.

He had already loosened his cravat and was in the process of wrenching his shirt off while she was still trying to unzip her dress.

'Turn around.' The gruff demand was an instant turn-on and she did as she was told.

The heat of his hands scorched the bare skin of her back as he unzipped her. When she was about to step out of her dress, his fingers deftly undid her strapless bra. Emmy's pulse quickened at the intimacy, and when he began to kiss the skin at her neck, she almost went into cardiac arrest. She fought to breathe normally despite her release from the restrictions of her bridesmaid's outfit. It, along with her underwear scaffolding, fell to the floor, leaving her standing in nothing but her panties.

Sam remained behind her, kissing his way along her shoulders, and cupping her breasts in his strong hands. He teased her nipples with his thumbs and forefingers until they were aching with need as much as the rest of her body.

Still, Sam continued the torturous exploration of her body with his hands. Slipping one under the lacy fabric of her remaining underwear to stroke her where she needed him most. She was leaning back against him, relying on his support as he let his fingers ease that ache inside her. Filling her, circling her and driving her to distraction.

Emmy turned her head, searching for his mouth, wanting to feel him everywhere at once. Sam took the cue from her and unbuttoned his trousers, dropping them onto the floor along with his boxers. Of course she looked, and she was not disappointed.

Sam kept in shape—she knew that. He jogged, and he played football, and it showed in every taut, lean muscle. Seeing him turned on looking at her naked body simply made her want him all the more. Before she knew it, he was backing her towards the bed, at the same time kissing and squeezing her tight. They fell down onto the mattress smiling and giggling in between the kisses, gasps and moans.

Emmy wanted to believe that this encounter was the culmination of a lifetime of wanting each other but she was not that naïve. This was just about sex and as long as she remembered that, her heart would survive having Sam for one night, before losing him again.

Primped and preened for her role in the wedding, this was the best she would ever look. Likely the best she would ever feel, with Sam kissing her all over, and not having to pretend to be anyone other than who she was to get him here. The only person she was trying to fool was herself if she thought having him just once could ever be enough.

CHAPTER TWO

Three months later

EMMY HAD FINISHED typing up her patient's details but took a few minutes to enjoy the luxury of sitting down. She had been on her feet all afternoon and no amount of cushioning in her trainers could ease the aching feet which came as part of the job.

She fished the cereal bar out of her pocket, broke a piece off and shoved it into her mouth.

'Hungry?' Shelley, one of her colleagues, joined her at the nurse's station to collect the information on her next patient.

'Always. I think I'm going to burst out of this uniform soon.' Since hitting puberty, Emmy had always struggled with anything fitted, her bust straining the fabric to breaking point. These days she was sure it was only a matter of time before all the stitches in the seams of her tunic gave way and left her in nothing more than her support underwear.

'You need to stop being in denial about this. It's happening. Give in to the inevitable, get a bigger size and try to be as comfortable as possible.'

'I'm not sure I'm ready to accept it yet.'

'Don't you think it's too late for that? When's your first scan?'

'Next week.' When that wriggling jelly bean appeared on the screen there would be no choice but to acknowledge there was a baby on the way. She was going to be a mother and that meant facing up to all the challenges that would bring.

The huge responsibility of another life was something her own parents had not been truly prepared for. Though Emmy intended to do everything in her power to raise a happy, well-adjusted child, there was that ever-present anxiety that she simply would not measure up. She had always wanted to have that chance to raise a family of her own, the right way. With unconditional love. However, her hopes for the relationship she would have with her child did not take away the fear of getting it wrong.

It was impossible to work in a field like paediatrics and not realise your potential as a caring mother figure, but worry had cancelled out her desire of having children and making up for the wrongs done to her in her early life. Even if she had found Mr Right, Emmy might have let her parents' mistakes overrule that maternal instinct she knew was deep inside her. Perhaps it was better things had turned out the way they had now there was no way back. Whatever happened with Sam, she was having this baby. It could be her last chance to be a mum and it was a blessing, despite the complicated circumstances.

Her hang-ups about parenting and her own upbringing were part of the reason she was yet to share the happy news with the father. She needed to get her head around everything before dealing with Sam's misgivings or issues about having his own children. After all, he had not had the greatest childhood either and chances were he was going to have to work through a lot of personal demons too before accepting his new role.

'Who's going with you?' Shelley perched on the edge of the desk, settling in for the interrogation Emmy knew was coming. Despite being a couple of years younger than her, Shelley acted like a concerned parent at times. If she was not worrying about Emmy getting home safely after a late shift, she was fretting over her getting ripped off by every con man in London apparently waiting for 'soft touches' like her. Emmy put it down to Shelley having grown up in the city and considering herself more streetwise than the country bumpkin working alongside her.

If Shelley had been at David's wedding, she would never have let Emmy sleep with Sam and completely turn her life upside down.

Even if Shelley could not have convinced her it was a bad idea, she would probably have reminded her to be safe and use protection. Emmy's current predicament was entirely her own fault. Carried away in the moment her fantasy had come true, the reality of pregnancy had not seemed possible. Until a few weeks later with the shock of a positive test.

'No one. I don't need anyone. I'm going to be doing this on my own anyway. I may as well get used to it.' It had been her decision entirely to keep the baby. Sam had made it clear he did not want anything more than a tumble in bed with her at the time. A baby together was the opposite of no-strings sex. She had got what she wanted and would have to live with the consequences. It did not seem fair to derail his successful career with a responsibility he never asked for. Most of all, Emmy could not bear the thought of her child growing up knowing it was unwanted by one of its parents. She knew the consequences of living with that stigma and would never inflict it on another innocent child.

Shelley folded her arms and tightened her mouth into a disapproving pout. 'I thought you were going to start telling people. They're going to notice soon anyway. You're pregnant, it's nothing to be ashamed about.'

Except she was. When she had imagined having a family of her own she never expected to do it without a partner who loved her sharing the experience. Emmy had always felt alone but at least there were going to be two of them from this moment forward. She rubbed her hand over her belly, which, these days, was a result of more than her sweet tooth.

Up until now she had let everyone believe she had simply put on a few extra pounds. They would not be noticed on a girl like her.

Only, in another month or so, it would be obvious this was more than a cake baby.

'I told those who needed to know.'

'Such as?' Shelley raised an eyebrow, not content to let her skimp on the details.

'You...'

'Because I figured it out for myself. One month you're playing bridesmaid at your brother's wedding and the next you've got your head stuck down the toilet bowl every morning.'

At that stage Emmy really had been in denial, convinced it was food poisoning, a virus or a sudden allergy to chocolate making her ill. It did not seem possible that after years of lusting after Sam she was having his baby. Without ever having the luxury of a relationship with him. The result of a wedding hook-up made it sound more sordid than the experience had actually been. Not that either of them had hung around to cuddle afterwards, and had gone back to the evening reception as though the world had not just rocked beneath them.

'I told management and human resources.' Forced to let them know in case she was put in a position which might have jeopardised the pregnancy. It also meant she could have her appointments and scans without having to make up excuses for her absence.

'What about David? Or the rest of your family? The father?'

Emmy shook her head at all three, waiting for a tut after every denial. 'I'm not ready to have those conversations yet.' If ever. It had crossed her mind about never going home again and raising her baby in secret but that was the fear talking. They might not be blood but the Jenningses were still her family and the time would come when she would need their support. She hoped she would get it. At least the twins were not at the stage of starting families of their own or her baby might have had difficulty getting her parents' attention, the way Emmy had. Competing against her sisters was not something she had anticipated after being adopted but that was what had happened when the twins' needs had seemed to come before her own in the household. She wanted her child to have better. To be accepted and loved equally as anyone else in the family. Again, that worry of things that had happened in the past was preventing her from moving forward.

'Well, you've got six months before you drop the baby bombshell on them so maybe you should start working on your speeches. Beginning with the father. Even if he isn't interested, he has a right to know.' Shelley handed her a notebook and pen before she collected her files and went back onto the wards.

Emmy knew she was right, but she could not bring herself to explode Sam's life just yet. The weight of guilt was pressing hard on her shoulders over the fact she had kept this secret from him for three months, without having to see or hear his disappointment too when she did finally tell him. He did not do commitment, she had known that from the start, but he no longer had a choice or a say in the matter. What was a baby other than a permanent, lifetime commitment he never asked for?

Emmy never wanted to upset Sam's life or trap him into being tied to her for the rest of his days. He was going to hate her for this.

'We'll send you for some X-rays and see what's going on with that arm of yours.' Sam smiled, trying to reassure the young patient that there was nothing to be concerned about. At that age he knew what it was to worry about things beyond your control, unsure of the future.

At nine years old, Sam had been aware something was not right at home. His father worked away all the time, yet they never seemed to have any money. The feeling that all was not as it should be had eaten away at him, but he had been powerless to do anything. He could not even have confided his fears to his mother when she was struggling to keep them afloat. To all intents and purposes a single mum, given how much time his father spent away from home. Life became so utterly unbearable for her, and a distance had emerged between Sam and his mother and he had been forced to grow up quickly. Mature beyond his years when it came to financial and emotional matters and not through choice. Neither of his parents had been there during his formative years, and looking after number one had been a necessity to Sam because no one else had been around to do it for him.

Finding out his father had a second family, and that he had ineffectively split his time between both, had come as a shock to his mother but not to Sam. It explained a lot, even if it did not make the consequences any easier to live with.

'Thanks, Doctor.' Marcus's mum was on her feet before Sam had barely finished his consultation.

The boy did not return Sam's smile. He hardly acknowledged he had spoken. Marcus was a sullen sort of child. Understandable when he was in pain after his fall. Yet the behaviour seemed more fitting for a teenager. Something simply did not feel right about this patient and Sam was expert enough in his field to trust his instincts. Usually.

His recent decision-making might be called questionable by some.

'If you could wait here with Marcus, Mrs Moseley, I'll get someone to take you both down to X-ray.'

The woman plopped back down into the chair by her son's bedside with a frown, looking as though she would rather be anywhere else.

Sam understood hospitals were not everyone's favourite place to be but he did come across some family members who did not always think of their child's wants or needs first. He also knew from personal experience. Treating their illness as an inconvenience rather than being sympathetic to their little ones who clearly needed reassurance and comforting for the duration of their hospital stay unfortunately was not a rare occurrence.

It never failed to irk him. Some parents, including his father, were too selfish to have had children. Never putting them first. That was why he had decided a long time ago family life was not for him. He would not inflict the sort of pain he had endured as a child on anyone else. No matter how unintentionally.

That selfishness was already in him when he devoted his time and energy completely into his work, often letting down partners who thought they deserved more of him too. It would be cruel to risk doing the same to an innocent child. This job often showed him how that turned out and it was not a pleasant scenario he wished to partake in from the other side.

'I hope this isn't going to take long?' Mrs Moseley took her phone from her pocket and began scrolling through her social media feed. No doubt one of those who posted their whereabouts to gain sympathy, he thought uncharitably.

He kept the smile pasted on as long as he could. 'I'll come back later to check in on you.'

Sam was determined to get to the bottom of Marcus's problems and was glad he had agreed to take on this short-term contract after all. He had worried about being too hasty in accepting the post soon after the wedding.

At the time he could not get Emmy out of his mind. They had not even had one full night together so he should have been able to get over her. He had always been fond of her and enjoyed her company but the three-year age difference when they were teenagers made so much more difference then, compared to now. Plus, Dave would have kicked his head in for even thinking of his sister in that way.

Seeing her after such a long time reminded him of how close they had been at one time, and she had looked gorgeous. In and out of the dress.

He shuffled through his notes as he walked down the corridor trying to take his mind elsewhere. Impossible. Especially now. If anything, sharing Emmy's bed had simply increased his desire to be with her. To the extent he had accepted a consultancy placement at the London City Hospital where he knew she worked. Something which now seemed impulsive given they had not spoken since the wedding.

In hindsight he could see that he had acted purely based on his desire to bed her again. Giving no thought to the consequences of turning up here out of the blue or considering if she would even want to see him again. Though, to his mind, their time together had been incredible and something worth repeating.

Emmy might be self-conscious around her sisters, but she was confident in bed and rightly so. Her soft skin and womanly curves were imprinted on his mind and body for ever. Yet, somehow, they had managed to rejoin the wedding reception that night without another word to each other.

He should have told her he would be working at the hospital when he accepted the post, but he hadn't. Convinced they would be in contact at some point where he could slip the information into the conversation. Now he was here, and it was only a matter of time before he ran into her. There was no way of knowing how she would react to his sudden appearance, or what he would do if she did not want him here.

Hell, he did not even know what he had hoped to achieve by coming. They were certainly not going to launch into a relationship and he could not expect Emmy to settle for being his sex buddy. She was worth more than that. The only reason he could come up with for accepting this job was that he simply wanted to see her again. He missed her.

With each step he took into her department, his doubts grew that being here was a good idea. He was no longer sure sleeping together had been one of his smarter decisions when it would change the nature of their relationship for ever.

It was too late to change his mind now. He was invested in his new patient and Emmy was at the end of corridor looking at him...

'Hey!' he shouted, watching her face turn ashen. Then she turned and fled in the opposite direction.

'Emmy! Wait!'

She could hear Sam calling her and knew there would be questions asked about why she was running from him but right now she needed space to breathe.

There was a conversation which needed to be had but Emmy had expected to do that on her own terms. Somewhere other than her workplace. Guilt crashed into her at full force now she was faced with the enormity of the secret she had been keeping from Sam. He had deserved to be told he was going to be a father from the moment she found out. To be involved in the decisions she had undertaken by herself and be a part of the process, but she had taken all of that away from him. Now the truth was going to have to come out on terms other than the ones she had planned. This was an ambush, and it was too late to scrabble back out of it.

Her pace gradually slowed when she realised how bizarre it would look to him to see her running away. Sam would have no idea why his sudden appearance here had sent her into such a panic.

'Emmy?' He called her name again, and she was forced to stop and talk to him. She would never outrun him anyway. Even if she got away from him today, he was so deeply embedded into her family life she could not hide the pregnancy from him for ever.

'Sam? What brings you here?' When Emmy finally faced him, it was with fake surprise.

'Didn't you hear me calling you?' He bounded up beside her and she noticed he was in his smart work attire, not the casual wear a passing visitor would have been sporting.

Her stomach lurched at the implications of that and having to lie straight to his face. 'No. I was in a world of my own. Sorry.'

There was a flicker of uncertainty across his forehead before he smiled. 'No problem. As long as you're not trying to avoid me?'

'Why on earth would I want to do that?' Her laugh was much too loud and high-pitched to be believable but she could not tell him the truth just yet. Not here or now.

'Well, uh, after the wedding, you know…'

It was the first time Emmy had ever seen him look remotely coy. The bloom of pink in his cheeks and the way he was shuffling his feet, unable to stand still, was endearing. He had never struck her as anything but a confident ladies' man. At least, not in adulthood.

Unless he was embarrassed by the whole

affair and regretting it had ever happened. That would make things even more complicated, or more clear-cut, if he decided he wanted nothing more to do with her. Since he had not called or texted during the intervening months, she assumed she had her answer. They had agreed that their time together would not be anything other than just sex, even though she had always known it would to her. Even more so now.

Regardless of Sam's ignorance of her feelings and current situation, the facts hardened her resolve not to get all mushy around him again. It would not do her any good.

'I'm a big girl. Don't worry, I think I can control myself around you.'

'That's not what I meant. I don't want things to be awkward between us.'

Like this? she thought.

'Why should they? It was a spur-of-the-moment thing. Over and done with.' Each lie that fell from her lips made her want to hold her stomach in a little more.

'You're my best mate's sister.'

This was not about her or her feelings at all. Sam was merely worried that it might affect his relationship with David. If she had been a bitter person she could easily have ended their friendship by confiding in her big brother about what had happened between them. Luckily for Sam, she cared too much about David to upset him by casting his best man in a very unfavourable light. He would not be pleased to learn that Sam had bedded his kid sister on his wedding night, got her pregnant and hoped they could forget it ever happened. If he knew, he would probably try and force them into a shotgun wedding, making Sam do the honourable thing. Not that Sam was aware of the outcome of their passionate tryst but they had not been as careful as they ought to.

'There's no need to get snarky about it, Emmy. We had a good time together, but I don't want to let what happened between us spoil my relationship with any of the family.'

It might be too late for that particular hope but only time would tell.

'Why are you here, Sam?' It certainly was not for her but she was curious and dismayed as to why he appeared to be working on her territory.

'I've taken up a consultant post. I'll be here a couple of days a week.' He seemed pleased with the news, but it was not what Emmy needed to hear. If he was going to be here on a permanent basis he would notice her condition pretty soon.

Bang went her plan to wait until the last minute to tell him he was going to be a father. She could not keep it from him for ever.

'That…that's great.' The words almost choked her.

'I probably should have told you. I know it'll come as a bit of a shock, but we've known each other for a long time. Hopefully we can carry on as we've always done.' His eyes were bright, his grin wide, but Emmy wanted to cry. Sam being here changed everything. She had been counting on the distance between them to help her manage. Now he was right on her doorstep there was no hiding. Not the pregnancy or her feelings about him. How was she going to be able to work here, seeing him around, if he did not want anything to do with her or the baby? It was his right to walk away when he owed her no commitment, but it was going to be more difficult to sever all ties if they were working in the same place.

'Of course. I'm sure I'll see you around.' She ended the conversation and the not-so-happy reunion. There was no point in carrying on this pretence that they had any kind of relationship now after sleeping together.

Deep down she had known it would change everything, but she had wanted him so much she ignored the risks. Sam never promised her anything other than a good time and delivered on it. He would not want this baby and that was primarily why she had delayed telling him. She would be lucky if he was still talking to her once he found out that not only was she carrying his baby, but she had kept it from him all this time.

Neither of them had planned this pregnancy, but now she was going to be a mum, Emmy wanted the best for her baby. To her mind that included stability, and parents who loved unconditionally and completely. By his own admission that was never going to include Sam.

She had let her baby down at the first hurdle.

CHAPTER THREE

SAM CONTINUED HIS rounds with a heavier heart than when he had started. The aim of coming to the city was partly to repair his relationship with Emmy. Perhaps even to pick up where they had left off at the wedding, but she appeared anything but happy to see him again.

It had not occurred to his giant ego that she would not want him in her life in any capacity. Yet she had made that obvious with her reaction after running into him. Emmy could not wait to get away from him. Which was going to make things strained between them at work and family get-togethers. One of which was scheduled for the following weekend.

It was Tom Jennings's seventieth birthday and Sam was not going to miss being part of

the celebrations, regardless of whatever re-
grets Emmy had about their time together.

'It's good to see you again, Marcus.' Sam
had taken a look at the X-rays he had requested and there were some concerns about
what they had revealed. The calcification on
the bone suggested an old fracture which had
not healed properly.

Sam suspected it was an injury which had
not been treated in hospital and the overriding question for him was why? He had to be
careful around the boy, who was withdrawn
enough as it was, and he did not want to say
or do anything to upset him further.

He perched on the side of the bed. 'Marcus,
the X-rays show an old fracture. Do you remember ever hurting your arm before?'

The boy bit his lip and shook his head.
Usually, children of this age were chatter-
boxes or trying to play football down the
corridors. Full of character. Marcus seemed
broken more than physically. Sam knew the
signs from a personal and professional prospective and was not happy sending him
home until they got to the bottom of this injury. It had made all the difference to him
having Emmy and David in his life when he

had gone through problems at home and he would be only too happy if he could make the same difference in another child's life.

'Are you sure? It must have hurt at the time.' A broken bone was not something easily dismissed. Especially if it had not been stabilised properly at the time.

'Doctor? Is everything all right?' Marcus's mother walked into the ward. Another person who did not look particularly pleased to see him. Surprising when it was his job to treat her son and make him better.

Sam got to his feet. 'I was just telling Marcus we found an old fracture on the X-ray which hasn't healed properly. That might be what's causing the problem. Do you remember how that could have happened?'

She shrugged her shoulders. 'He's a clumsy child. Always falling and bumping into things.'

'This would've been more painful than a mere bump.' He could see her hackles rising as he probed for more information, but it was necessary in case they had to inform social services about a possible safeguarding issue with the boy's home life.

'How am I supposed to know? He lies and

exaggerates. If you had kids of your own you'd know how difficult it is to figure out when they're genuinely ill and not faking it to get out of going to school.' With her arms folded and standing straighter, she was unsurprisingly defensive at the turn the conversation was taking. She was not to know if he had kids or not, and despite his own experiences and misgivings about being a parent, Sam was sure he would notice if his son had broken his arm.

Sam was about to point out a fracture should have been easier to diagnose than a sore throat but thought better of it. She would only clam up if he pushed any further. If he had suspicions about Marcus's situation at home—and he did—there were procedures to follow. He would have to voice his concerns if there was any sign of a life endangerment issue. Where children were concerned they could not take any chances and rightly so. Getting involved could make all the difference in a child's life if they were having a hard time of it and Sam should know.

'We're going to run a few more tests to make sure there's nothing serious going on, so we'll be keeping Marcus in overnight.' In these circumstances they would have to carry out a full safeguard medical assessment—a full skeletal survey along with a CT and MRI scan—to make sure there were no other injuries.

The 'concerned' parent tutted before taking up residence in the chair by the bed again.

'I'll call back and see how you're doing later, Marcus.' It was a promise, even if his mother was eyeing him warily as though he had just threatened her.

Sam was still wondering what was going on between the pair when he passed Emmy on the stairs, on his way to see another patient.

'Hey.' For a second he thought she was not even going to stop, never mind acknowledge him.

Then she paused halfway down the steps, with her hand on the rail, bracing herself before she spoke to him. It was not any more reassuring than if she had completely blanked him. For the life of him he did not know what he had done to make her hate him so much. He thought their time at the wedding had been amazing. Certainly nothing that should warrant the cold shoulder she appeared to be giving him lately. If she regretted anything, he hoped a civil discussion could have worked things out but he understood this was not the ideal venue to do that. It was better to stick to safer, more relevant topics. Such as the patient he had just left.

'Hey.' Emmy's returned greeting sounded more like resignation that she would have to talk to him. A long way away from the warm hugs and squeals she once gave upon seeing him. He was missing that side of Emmy as much as the passionate woman he had made love to only a few months ago.

'Um, Dave invited me to your father's birthday this weekend. I hope that's not going to be a problem?'

'You're coming, then?' There was no attempt to hide her disappointment at the news. Clearly she did not want him in any part of her life.

It would be a shame to let what had happened spoil things between them and Sam wished they could stay amicable. The bond he had with Emmy was the closest thing to a relationship he'd ever had.

'Yes. You know he was like a second father to me growing up. I'll be there with bells on. Unless you've a good reason for me not to come?' It was a direct challenge to her to tell him what was bothering her. Either she stopped trying to avoid him or explained once and for all why he should not continue to be involved with the family the way he had always been. He wanted to move past this awkwardness and get back to what they used to have together.

Her silence spoke volumes. She did not want him there but was not willing to tell him why.

Eventually she said, 'No. No reason. I suppose I'll see you there.'

If Sam had hoped for a repeat performance of the wedding night, he knew he was out of luck. There was no hint of flirtation or any evidence she liked him at all now. He could not fathom what he had done for her to turn against him after all of this time.

When she went to walk on past him he had to ask, 'Did I do something to upset you, Em?'

Again she hesitated too long for her answer to be true. 'No.'

He had definitely done something. Whatever it was, he was determined to put it right.

'Emmy—'

His plea to set things straight was lost in the sound of someone shouting for help from the children's ward. An emergency took priority over his private life and everything else when a child's life could be at stake.

Emmy continued on down the stairs and he turned back too, both rushing to the source of the commotion.

'Nurse! Help. He's fitting.'

Emmy was at the child's side before Sam got there, checking there was nothing blocking the airways, or anything around which could hurt the boy having the seizure as his mother watched, horrified and helpless.

'Oxygen.' Sam grabbed the mask and placed it over the child's mouth to help him breathe, and Emmy checked her watch.

'This is Liam. Twelve years old. Epileptic,' she said, brushing the hair from the boy's eyes whilst timing the event. If the fit lasted more than five minutes they would have to administer buccal midazolam to try and stop it. Until then all they could do was reassure the boy everything would be fine.

'It's going to be okay, Liam. We'll get you through this one.' There was that calm, soothing tone she used to use on him, when he would come to the Jennings place, upset after another problem at home. No doubt caused by his father. It was no wonder she had gone into nursing when she had always looked after everyone else. Her kindness could not be taught at school. Emmy was a natural carer.

Liam's tremors gradually began to lessen and Sam was glad Emmy had been on hand so they could act quicker. She likely knew more about every child in here than was written in their files. He was sure she brought a smile to the faces of everyone on the ward. At the same time doing everything she could to make them comfortable as possible, while trying to get them back on their feet.

Sam only hoped he had not messed things up for her at work by inserting himself back into her life.

Once Liam was stabilised, and the adrenaline was no longer pumping so vehemently in his veins, Sam tried again with Emmy.

'Are you ready for a cuppa after that?' he asked as they left the ward.

This time her reply was instant. 'Yes, please.'

Helping Liam get through his latest seizure had taken all of the fight out of Emmy. She got tired quickly these days and she needed her energy to hide her condition from Sam. Right now, she could do with a timeout from having to think and a seat to take the weight off her feet. Something sweet to boost her blood sugar would be welcome too. Sam had caught her in a moment of vulnerability, but she could not avoid him for ever. He would be part of her life in a big way from now on, whether either of them wanted that or not.

However, she was going to wait until after her dad's birthday to break the news. She did not want to bring any drama to the festivities. If she told Sam now about the baby it would come out at home too, and she could do without the derision from her sisters over her current predicament. There was time enough after she had her scan to make sure everything was all right first. Another chance for Emmy to beat herself up about shutting Sam out of the pregnancy, even if she thought it was probably for the best.

'Coffee? Tea?' Sam asked as they joined the queue in the canteen. He knew she was partial to both. What he was unaware of was her decision to go caffeine-free for the duration of the pregnancy.

'A glass of milk, please.'

Her request stunned him momentarily. 'Okay. I'll get the drinks if you want to go and get us a table?'

Under other circumstances she might have protested about paying her way, but her feet hurt. 'Thanks.'

She left him to pay and relaxed as best she could in the hard plastic chair, aware that things would only get harder over the next few months. Maternity leave and when she would be taking it was the first of many decisions she would have to make as a prospective single mum.

'One glass of fresh milk for m'lady.' With the flourish of a wine waiter in a high-class establishment, Sam set the drink in front of her.

He was trying, bless him, and if it was not for the repercussions of their night of fun she would enjoy the company. As it was, he put her on edge, knowing he was going to feel differently around her soon. Being faced with a responsibility he had never asked for was not something he was going to appreciate. Along with being kept in the dark because she did not want to face reality.

'Thank you.'

'Are you okay after that little drama? If you don't mind me saying, you look tired.' He produced a snack pack of biscuits from his pocket and Emmy pounced on it.

'You're a lifesaver. I think my blood sugar's a little low. You know how it is…skipping meals always catches up with you.'

'Exactly why you should be taking care of yourself, Em. It's a demanding job and it takes its toll. Lucky for you, I know you've got a sweet tooth.'

'Yes, Doctor.' It was nice to hear the concern in his voice for her and she wished it was related to the fact she was carrying his baby.

He laughed and shook his head at her. 'Who would ever have thought we'd both end up going into medicine and specialising in paediatrics at that?'

Emmy murmured her agreement, deciding not to tell him she had followed him into medicine because his passion for it had been intoxicating. In listening to Sam's desire to help others, she had believed going into nursing would somehow bring them closer too. That dream of a lovestruck teenager had become the nightmare of an adult who had not made any better life decisions.

'Our troubled childhoods might have played a part. We want to help kids who are having a hard time of it.' That much was true. Her whole reason for being in this department was to try and make life better for the youngsters who had been dealt a rough hand at such a young age.

'I suppose so. I've never thought of it in that way. We might actually have something to thank our feckless parents for after all.' The way he gulped down a mouthful of hot coffee told her he did not believe that any more than she did. They had become essential workers despite their absent parents, who deserved absolutely no credit for the way their children had turned out.

The dull buzz of a pager went off, and as soon as Sam checked it, he was on his feet, taking one last swig of coffee. 'I've got to go but I'll see you on Sunday, yeah?'

'Yes,' she confirmed, as their break came to an end and her mind and body filled with foreboding over their next planned encounter.

Intuition told her it was not going to be as pleasant and relaxed as the last ten minutes together and could change things between them, and her family, for ever.

* * *

For the whole train journey to her parents' house, Emmy had been praying that Sam would have a work emergency or get caught up in traffic. Anything to prevent him attending the celebrations. Being close to the family was great when she was younger and looked forward to his visits. Now, it was an inconvenience at a time when she would rather not see him. It was bad enough they were working together without socialising too. Every meeting raised the possibility of him finding out about their surprise baby and her having to own up to keeping it to herself for three months. It was difficult to know if the unplanned pregnancy or her betrayal would have a bigger impact on Sam. Emmy never wanted to hurt him but knew that was exactly what would happen once he found out about everything.

He had offered to drive her, but she could not bear the thought of a long car journey when they would invariably bring up the subject of David's wedding night. The memory of which she would always treasure but was also a reminder of her uncertain future.

As Emmy made the short journey from the

train station to the house on foot, her nerves began to get the better of her. Family occasions always made her fret over what to wear and her appearance when she wanted to make a good impression. The pressure was twofold today, knowing Sam would be here too, oblivious to his impending fatherhood.

In the end she had gone with a sunny yellow, empire-line dress which hugged her bosom and skimmed over her tummy, in an effort to detract from any changes in her body. The addition of a sunflower clip in her hair was projecting a bright countenance she was not feeling.

On the way to the door she took a deep breath and rapped. Whether it was due to good manners or an instilled sense of not completely belonging, she did not simply let herself in, but waited for someone to open the door for her.

'Don't stand on ceremony, Emmy, come in.'

She was glad it was her dad who answered, genuinely happy to see her.

'Happy birthday.' She flung her arms around him and hugged him tight. The squeeze in return made her feel more secure than she had in months.

'Thanks, sweetheart. It's good to see you.'

She handed over the card and present she had chosen so carefully and hung her coat up in the hall.

'So, uh, who's here?' There could have been a hundred people inside but there was only one person's presence she was concerned about.

'Oh, it's just a quiet family dinner. I didn't want a big fuss.' That was her dad, humble and unassuming, but unhelpful when it came to her personal life.

'Hello, stranger. I haven't seen you since the wedding.'

For a heart-stopping moment she thought the strong arm around her shoulders was Sam's until David spoke.

'I was giving you newlyweds some privacy.' She kissed him on the cheek and took advantage at the chance of another hug. Goodness knew how he would react when he found out his best friend had got his little sister pregnant. Especially when Sam would not want the responsibility of the unplanned pregnancy.

'It's been nearly three months, sis. You're welcome to come to our house anytime. There's no need to avoid us, we're family.'

Emmy could tell from his tone and the strength of his embrace he was worried about her feeling pushed out by Bryony. Given that was exactly what had happened when Lorna and Lisa had been born into the family.

Although nothing could have been further from the truth where Bryony was concerned. David's new wife brought him happiness and that was all she could ask for him.

He was right about one thing though: she had been avoiding him and talking about the wedding day, along with his best friend. Although that had proved pointless now Sam was working at her hospital.

'I know. I know. I've just been busy…with stuff.' Hormones, morning sickness, anxiety and sleepless nights worrying about the future or if she should have included Sam in everything earlier.

'Well, today you rest and enjoy. Your mother has been cooking all day.' Her father directed them towards the dining room where the rest of the family was already seated around the table, including Sam.

All the air seemed to escape her lungs at the sight of him sitting there.

'You're just in time, sweetheart,' her mother greeted her from the far end of the table, which was already laden with platters of food.

Despite all the hellos and smiles from her sisters as well, Emmy could not help but note they had started without her.

As if sensing her disappointment, Sam spoke up. 'I knew your train had just got in so we thought we'd have everything ready for your arrival.'

True or not, the explanation, along with the knowledge he had bothered to check on her train, eased a tiny bit of her trepidation.

'Get stuck in before everything goes cold. Roast beef, and your favourites, Yorkshire puddings. There's a seat beside Sam for you.'

Directed towards the empty chair, Emmy sat down and exchanged an awkward smile with Sam.

'Hey,' he said. Enough to make her blush.

'Hi.' She managed a brief sideways glance before sitting down and helping herself to slices of roast beef before David ate them all.

The room was momentarily filled with the

sound of the happy diners' chatter as they passed around the dishes piled high with food, and Emmy longed for it to stay that way.

'I can't remember the last time I had a home-cooked meal. It's usually something quick in between shifts.' Her appetite had not been quite the same lately. Certain strong-smelling foods made her stomach roll and her favourite curries were giving her heartburn too. It was small, simple meals these days, although she was trying to eat the right foods for the baby's sake.

'You've got to look after yourself, Emmy. Doesn't she, Sam?' For some reason her mother looked to him on the matter. Probably because he was a doctor, and in her eyes better qualified and more respected than a lowly nurse.

Emmy had always been proud of the job she did looking after the kids at the hospital, but her parents thought it beneath her. They were a very middle-class family and having money without being seen to labour hard for it seemed more acceptable than working with 'the great unwashed.' Her parents had a snobbish attitude when it came to mixing with the general public because their careers had been very much at the top of the pay scale. Although now retired, her father had been a successful investment banker, her mother a financial advisor, and it had been a long time since either of them had to worry about money. They did not understand why she would undervalue herself so much to work for the health service.

According to them she should have used her brains and gone into an office-based job where she could charge exorbitant rates simply for use of her time, like David the solicitor. Nursing was a poorly paid profession compared to his and the airy-fairy, social media 'influencers' her sisters proclaimed themselves to be. She had no issues with their make-up tutorials or vlogs about their travel adventures. They had not been as book smart as Emmy or David and she admired their ability to make a career from their interests. She simply did not understand why their paths were more acceptable than hers. Especially when Lorna and Lisa had borrowed money to set up their venture into the world of social media until they had sufficient paying subscribers and sponsors to fund their lifestyle. Emmy had never asked for a handout, nor had one been offered. Her sisters had asked for financial help from their parents to start their online business but Emmy had been aware from the moment she had professed an interest in nursing that they thought it a poor career choice with no prospects for significant financial gain. Money seemed to be their marker for stability in life and so Emmy did not want to further their concerns for her by getting into debt from the off.

Instead, she had worked where she could to get her through her nursing course and stood on her own two feet financially from the day she finished high school. Just one more example of the different standards separating her from her sisters.

Still, at least her mother was showing some concern for her welfare, even if the delivery stung.

'Yes. Yes, she does.' Sam smiled and went to pour her some wine. Emmy quickly covered the glass with her hand.

'Not for me, thanks. I'll stick with water.' She poured herself some from the jug in the centre of the table, ignoring the bemused looks around the table. Anyone would think she had a reputation when it came to alcohol simply because she had turned down one glass of wine.

'That's a beautiful dress. It's a lovely colour on you,' Bryony commented, oblivious to the sniggering going on around the table at Emmy refusing a drink. If everyone found it so unbelievable, she was going to have to look at her drinking habits when the baby was born. Unless this was merely another example of her family taking the opportunity to make fun of her.

'Thanks.' It was nice to have another woman onside when her sisters' compliments often hid a thinly veiled barb.

'Hmm. Not sure it's your style though,' Lorna piped up on cue, ready to spoil Emmy's mood as she nibbled a piece of a carrot.

'Yeah. It does nothing for your figure. Have you put on weight?' Lisa was as direct as expected.

'Now, girls, it's not Emmy's fault she hasn't inherited my good metabolism. You should think yourself lucky.' Her mother did not even realise how incredibly insensitive she too was being, pointing out yet again that Emmy was not biologically one of the family. It was entirely possible she had passed on more than the ability to stay slim to the twins when their acerbic tongues sounded suspiciously like their parents' at times.

Emmy should be used to the comments by now and, usually, she did not react, but her hormones were making her more sensitive at the moment. Tears were already blurring her vision at the fact she was not allowed to enjoy a birthday meal without criticism.

Their parents would never dare criticise the wonder twins and that was part of the problem. They had always been allowed to say or do whatever they pleased without retribution and had grown from spoiled children into mean-spirited adults who got their kicks putting others down. Emmy in particular.

'I think you look lovely, Emmy.' Sam reached out and squeezed her hand in solidarity, but it only furthered her regret about coming here at all.

'Hang on, no wine…extra weight…you're not pregnant, are you?' Lorna snorted at the idea and set her sibling off too. Either the notion of Emmy becoming a mother, or that someone had slept with her, apparently was hysterically funny.

Heat rose in Emmy's cheeks and she could

not find the strength to deny the possibility with a blatant lie. Her delay in spouting a witty comeback told a tale.

The collective sound of gasps, dropped cutlery and astonished laughter was almost deafening. She did not dare look any of them in the eye. Especially Sam, who she was sure was currently glaring a hole into the side of her head.

'Emmy? Is this true?' Her father's stern voice broke through the humiliation of her worst nightmare come true. His vocal disapproval made her feel as though she had besmirched the family name like some unmarried teen mum from the fifties when such a thing was considered a scandal. These days, her situation was not unusual, and better accepted. In other circles, apparently.

No, this was not how she wanted anyone to find out, overshadowing what should have been a joyous occasion, but Emmy knew there was never going to be a good time.

She could already feel her parents' disappointment emanating in waves.

Emmy lowered her head and gave a small nod. Her mother cried out. She was a grown woman but still their daughter, pregnant and without a partner. It was natural they should have concerns but it was not the end of the world for any of them. She only wished they could skip the shock factor and move straight to the acceptance stage.

David cleared his throat. 'Congratulations, sis. I mean, I thought we'd be the ones having the first grandkids but I know you'll make a great mum.' Her brother's attempt to make her feel better was undone when her father spoke.

'Who's the father?' At least he hadn't asked if she knew who the father was, which was something the twins would likely have come up with.

They were unusually quiet. Probably realising they did not need to say or do anything when she had caused maximum damage already.

'I didn't mean to spoil your birthday,' she said, quietly.

An uneasy quiet descended around the table as they waited for the big reveal like some awful TV talent show, delaying the name in order to increase the drama. Only in this case they could do with dialling down the drama. No one was coming out of this a winner.

All of a sudden Sam scraped his chair back and stood up. 'I'm the father and we're getting married.'

Her 'Pardon me?' was drowned out by the loud squeals of delight from all around.

Before Emmy knew what was happening, everyone was congratulating them and shaking hands across the table. Meanwhile, Sam was grinning like an idiot and she was left bewildered by what was happening.

'When did this happen?'

'I'm so happy for the two of you.'

'You kept that quiet.'

'Our first grandchild…'

The effusive congratulations were a stark contrast to the previous feeling she was about to be disowned, and the only difference had been Sam's apparent involvement. It made her wonder if he was considered more of a son than she was their daughter, or if she was somehow more acceptable as part of a couple with him. Albeit a complete fabrication.

Emmy had no idea what Sam was playing at but was at a loss to do anything other than sit there and pretend with him. It seemed better to go along with it for now than to call it out for the lie it was and spoil the day again. They could talk it over later and she would put him straight on a few matters. Number one being that he was under no obligation to her or the baby. Despite what her family might think.

CHAPTER FOUR

SAM SLUMPED BACK in his chair in a daze. What on earth had he just done? He looked at Emmy, who was staring at him, mouth and eyes wide open, silently asking him the same question. All he could offer was a pitiful shrug.

Everything seemed to have happened at once, giving him no time to think about what he was doing before he had got up and addressed the whole Jennings family on their behalf. As though he was speaking for Emmy too. When in reality he did not even have ownership of the words, never mind her or the baby.

The baby. Emmy's baby. He had not even been mentioned. Yet he had fronted up and accepted responsibility. Why? It could have been out of guilt, knowing he had done the wrong thing by her and the family, taking advantage of their close bond for one hot night with Emmy. Perhaps it was his natural instinct to protect her when the twins had ganged up on her. A pattern which had repeated itself over time. It could have been self-preservation, knowing if David found out they had slept together he would have killed him, save for the idea of marriage. Judging by the reaction of the majority around the table, he had made the right decision. Bar the supposed newly engaged couple who must look miserable as sin. Marriage was a long way from the 'just sex' he and Emmy had agreed upon. Sam did not even know if the baby was his, simply assuming she had not been with anyone since because he hadn't.

For all he knew she could have been in a relationship with the father or been artificially inseminated because she did not want any male interference in her life. He had gone steamrollering over her news without a thought to anyone, including himself. Marriage and children were not things he had ever wanted. Something he should have given more consideration to before getting carried away with Emmy at the hotel.

If the baby was his, Sam did not want her

castigated for something he had been a part of. She did not deserve to take the flak on her own after fighting so hard to be accepted into this family. When it came to Emmy, some-one he had been close to for a long time, he was willing to sacrifice his independence if it meant making her feel secure in some small way. He could not in good conscience have sat back and let her be vilified for what had been a very special time to him. In standing up like that, he had been defending that time they had shared together, as well as giving her some support. Even if she had not asked him for it.

'You're actually going to be my real bro now.' David gave Sam another slap on the back when he walked past.

At this rate he would be stooped over, his skin red raw, at the end of the night with all of the physical congratulations.

'I guess so,' Sam replied uneasily, his con-science beginning to bother him.

All of this could come crashing down around him at any point if Emmy decided to call him out on his deception. So far she had not contradicted his story and gone along with the news. Most likely because she was either in shock, or it was easier to simply play along for now.

They had a lot to discuss. Apart from his spontaneous engagement and parenting announcement, there was the small matter of paternity. This could very well be his baby and that was going to change his life for ever.

He thought of his father and the neglected children he had spawned over the years along with the heartbroken women left behind. Sam swore never to be that person, yet he had acted with Emmy in the same selfish, reckless way. Thinking only of his own pleasure and conveniently forgetting the possible consequences. Even if Emmy appeared to have experienced high levels of pleasure at the time too.

There was not much opportunity for him to speak to her alone over the course of the afternoon. Although the dark looks she shot him every now and then said perhaps that was not such a bad thing. He knew he was in serious trouble when she actually accepted his offer of a lift home.

'Why? Why would you do that?' she asked, waving goodbye to the family as he drove away from the house.

'I don't know. I suppose it seemed like the right thing to do in the moment.' He could not explain what had happened to her when he hadn't figured it out completely himself.

'*Congratulations* or *Are you stupid?* seem to be the other available options. "We're getting married" was a more extreme reaction than I'd expected.' Emmy's hands were clasped tightly in her lap and he wondered how hard she was trying not to slap him.

'I didn't appreciate the way they were speaking to you.' A pathetic excuse, but the truth, nonetheless. He hated the way the twins ganged up on her and wished the rest stuck up for her more. Their ignorance of the pain their jibes caused Emmy only widened the distance between them all. It was not Sam's place to tell them how to behave, and even if he did, he doubted it would make any difference other than to alienate him from the family. Emmy would argue it was not his place to lie on her behalf either, but the deed was done now. The family of his best friend believed they were getting married and starting a family. The thought alone was enough to bring him out in a cold sweat.

'I was merely trying to keep you respectable.' Even as he said it, Sam knew the joke would fall flat. As confirmed by the sharp intake of Emmy's breath next to him.

'Pardon me? Do you really think I need a fake fiancé, or a man of any description, to give my life meaning?'

'I didn't mean—' His attempt to apologise was drowned out by her justified indignation at his ill-judged comment.

'I am a qualified nurse. An independent woman. I can raise this baby on my own. It won't make me any less of a mother or a human if I don't have a man at my side.'

It had not crossed Sam's mind that she would happily go it alone with the baby. He could walk away with a clear conscience if that was what he chose to do. Except Emmy was the last person he would bail on.

'You're all of those things and I'm sure you'll be a fantastic mum. I was merely saying I could help provide more stability for the child. We both know how important that is for a good start in life.' The more he talked about it, the more his proposition made sense. It might have started out as an impulsive re-action to her news and the Jenningses' attitude to it but he was beginning to think it was the answer.

He never planned on becoming a father, but would stand by Emmy and the baby, no matter what. It was his fault for not being careful and he had no intention of following in his father's footsteps. This baby needed a dad and needed to know it was loved and wanted. Not a mistake he regretted or could ignore.

'Yes, well, we can't change the past. Nor can we pretend we have a future together. The best I can hope for is that the excitement dies down after a few weeks and I'll come clean or tell them we broke up. Anything to stop them planning the wedding of the year.'

Clearly Emmy needed more time to get on board with the idea.

'It is my baby, then? Obviously I'll be there for you no matter what. It's just…good to know. Wow. I'm gonna be a dad.' Having the paternity confirmed made it all too real and only convinced him that he had been just in his actions, if impulsive.

Emmy rolled her eyes at him. 'Of course you're the father. I don't make a habit of one-night stands. Wait…you did all that without being one hundred percent sure this was your child I'm carrying?'

He nodded, having difficulty in forming words when there was so much for him to process. 'So you're...'

Emmy stared at him, waiting for him to complete the sentence, until they eventually did so together.

'Three months pregnant.'

Sam paused again. That was a quarter of a year. All that time Emmy had known she was pregnant with his baby and had not told him. Why? Would she ever have sought him out to tell him he was going to be a father if he had not shown up at the hospital?

He fought to maintain his concentration on the road as his thoughts and feelings were running at maximum power trying to make sense of Emmy's actions. Most of which were veering towards him being purposely left out of the loop and how much that pained him.

'Didn't you trust me, Emmy?'

'Hmm?'

'I'm just trying to figure out why you didn't tell me you were pregnant. You've had three months for goodness' sake.' He was trying and failing to keep himself in check. His raised voice giving away something of his hurt that she had not contacted him at all during that time.

Emmy sighed. 'It's complicated. Obviously neither of us expected this to happen and, well, we've both got our own lives to lead.'

'That's an excuse. We're both going to be parents. You should have involved me.' He did not know what difference it would have made to Emmy or the baby, if any, had she told him from the moment she had a positive test result. Hell, he would have been there for her as soon as she had thought a pregnancy was a possibility. What he did know was that he would have felt better knowing she could confide her fears in him. As it was, this secret meant she had not trusted him.

'I had a lot to figure out for myself. We've both had messed-up families and it worries me about the sort of parents we'll make.'

'You'll be an amazing mum, and though I understand your reservations about me on the parenting score, it doesn't change the fact that I am going to be the baby's dad. Don't shut me out any more than you already have. I know what it's like to have an absentee father and it's not fair to inflict that on an innocent child simply because you think I'm going to suck as much as my own parents.' Although he had never seen himself taking on the traditional role of a husband and father, the potential for Emmy to deny him now made his heart ache more than he thought it would for the life he could have with her and their baby.

He and Emmy made a good team, and could learn from their parents' mistakes. Sam wanted the chance to prove himself now that fate had decided fatherhood was in his future after all.

'It wasn't that… I felt guilty about keeping the news to myself but I also couldn't bear the thought of ruining your life. You've always been honest about not wanting to be tied down by family life, yet here we are…a baby on the way and a marriage proposal all in one afternoon.' She attempted a smile, but Sam could see through it to the sadness Emmy was trying to mask.

He could only hope he would do better by their baby when he had already upended Emmy's world with his selfish, reckless behaviour with his rampant libido.

'Look, we're in this together. We'll work something out.' Although he was saying all the right things, Sam was not jumping up and down with glee about the situation.

Sure, he was hurt and rightly so, but a bruised ego was not the same as an excited father-to-be.

Emmy needed to lie down in a dark room somewhere. Today had been too much. An overwhelming display of emotions from those around her.

'Why did you tell everyone we were getting married anyway? It seemed a little drastic. Especially for you.'

When Sam had first jumped up to defend her honour, she had been stunned into silence by the gesture. No one had ever stood up for her like that, but she had also known it was an act for her family's sake. By the time she realised what Sam was up to, everyone was already celebrating and accepting them as a couple. Something she had been striving for her whole life and only achieved with Sam on board. She wished it were true.

The only real part of this was the little one growing inside her. Everything else had been made up to impress her parents.

In an ideal world she would happily marry Sam and raise their baby together. However, this seemed like a sick joke. Teasing her with something she had dreamed about as a love-infatuated teen, when it was nothing more than a knee-jerk reaction to her news.

At least he had offered to do the right thing by her, regardless of the baby's parentage. It left an ember of hope burning that there was something more than chivalry behind the suggestion.

'It was a heat-of-the-moment thing. Expected.' Just like that, Sam poured a bucket of cold water over the flicker of hope, making it spit and hiss until there was nothing left but the muddy ashes of her dreams. She was done being a charity case, or the consolation prize for the real thing.

Despite Sam's hurt about the secret she had kept from him for so long, by the time they pulled up outside her house she knew she would have to do this alone. Forcing him to be in her life, or him thinking he had to be involved through some sense of duty, would not be fair on either of them. Not least for her when she would always be hoping there was something more behind Sam accepting responsibility for their 'mistake.' She was facing a lifetime of unrequited love and longing if he ended up being in his child's life for the long haul.

'Once you've slept on it, you'll realise what a mistake this whole thing was between us. You don't need to marry me or help raise a child you never wanted simply because you would feel guilty otherwise. I see no point in prolonging our agony for ever, Sam. I don't want or expect anything from you or anyone else. I never have.' She got out of the car, slamming the door on his plea for her to wait. The sobs started before he had driven away.

So much for her being stronger on her own.

Sam had slept on it. At least, he had lain in his bed, his mind whirring, trying to process everything. The frightening prospect of becoming a father and any urge to bolt from the responsibility was overridden by his sense of loyalty to Emmy and the innocent child they were about to bring into the world.

They had both had unhappy childhoods and it had affected all of their future relationships. He did not want to inflict that pain onto another generation.

She had given him an out, but now Emmy had had time to calm down and reflect on his suggestion, he was hoping to talk her round to his way of thinking.

They used to have a good relationship and if they could get that back it would be a good basis for a marriage, as well as providing security for their unborn child. Whatever she thought of him, he was not going to leave her to deal with this on her own. After the Jenningses' performance around the dinner table when she had broken the news, he was not sure they would be there for her at all. It would not be fair to walk away and leave Emmy to cope on her own simply because he had not planned for this. Neither of them had but it was happening, nonetheless. He might have to work hard at it, but Sam was not his father. He was not going to walk out when the mood took him or because he did not want to face up to his actions.

Once he had finished his ward rounds, he sought Emmy out, intending to discuss the matter with her again. He was not going to let her shut him out because she was trying to be a martyr and save him the hassle of a surprise pregnancy. Marriage was extreme but it would also be a symbol of his commitment to her and the baby.

As he was walking towards her department, he caught sight of her leaving, coat on, with her handbag over her shoulder. He rushed over, keen to catch her before she exited the building altogether.

'Hey, Emmy, I didn't realise you were finishing early today. I was hoping to catch you for a chat.'

'I…er…have an appointment.' She would not quite meet his eye and a swell of concern suddenly rose from the pit of Sam's stomach into his throat.

'Is everything all right, with you and the baby?' He was only coming to terms with the prospect of impending fatherhood and anything threatening that now would be too cruel.

She sighed. 'I have my first scan this afternoon.'

The unease subsided, only to be replaced with that now familiar hurt that she had either purposely kept the appointment from him or had not thought he would like to have been included in this important event.

'Can I come with you?' He would not impose where he was not wanted, but at the same time he had a right to be there to see his baby.

Emmy shrugged. 'If you want but I'm happy to go on my own.'

It was not the effusive 'Yes' he wanted. His intention had only been to support her, but when she was treating him as an inconvenience, Sam wondered if he was needed at all.

'I'd like to. If that's okay with you?' The idea of seeing their baby on the screen for the first time was something he could not pass up. Even if she had failed to mention it to him before now. It was a once-in-a-lifetime experience which would never be repeated and he should be there to witness it.

'You are the father, I suppose.' She started walking away, leaving it to him to follow her to the maternity wing.

Once she gave her name at reception, they both took their seats in the waiting room with more expectant couples. Sam saw a clear distinction between them and the other prospective parents in the room. Those dads-to-be were very tactile, holding hands or rubbing their partners' bellies with a reassurance they were in this together.

He had a feeling if he tried that with Emmy

it would earn him a punch on the nose for daring to as much as touch her again. It was natural to want to give her the same comfort and say that everything would be all right, but Emmy clearly regretted being with him in the first place. He had a lot of work to do to convince her to have him around, never mind persuade her that marriage was a good idea.

'Emma-Louise Jennings?' The nurse called her through, and Sam refrained from any comments over the use of her full name. There was a way to go before they would get back to that level of teasing each other again.

No one really knew him at the hospital yet in a professional capacity so he should not embarrass her too much by being here. How their work and personal relationships were going to play out in the future he did not know. All he could do was stand in the corner whilst Emmy got settled onto the bed, knowing she would not appreciate his help or a reminder he was here.

'If you could just lift your top up, I'll put some gel on your tummy.' The sonographer tucked some protective paper down the waistband of her trousers before squeezing the gloopy liquid generously onto Emmy's stomach. Sam was sure he could see a little more rounding in that area, although he would never say it or he might be in danger of losing vital parts of his anatomy.

Emmy was watching the screen as the sonographer ran the scanner over her belly. Sam could tell she was anxious by the way she was clenching her fists, tense, waiting for proof the baby was okay. He felt the same.

'Do you hear that?' With a turn of some knobs and some technical wizardry, the room filled with a fast, rhythmic beat.

'Yes.' Emmy sounded breathless, transfixed by the images on the monitor.

'That's baby's heart, strong and clear.'

Emmy let out an excited gasp and turned to look at him, the love for the baby shining brightly in her eyes. He smiled back at her, his heart racing as fast as the baby's. An exhilarating but terrifying time. He had not expected to be anxious but here he was, holding his breath waiting for confirmation their baby was fine.

'And this is your baby. Why don't you come closer, Dad?' As more buttons were pressed, a steady black-and-white image was captured on the screen and Sam was beckoned to be part of the event.

When he moved closer to Emmy he could see the tears of happiness glinting in her eyes. Then she reached out for his hand and gave it a squeeze.

Perhaps she might just let him be part of her life after all.

Emmy had been caught up in the moment. Overwhelmed with love for the little grey splodge on the screen. Otherwise she would have stopped herself reaching out for Sam. He was only holding her hand and sitting in on the scan because he knew it was expected of him. She did not see the point in forcing him to do these things. It would not take long for him to realise it was not the life he wanted, raising an unplanned child with a woman he did not love. She would not make the mistake of thinking he would be in this for ever.

'Can I get a copy of the picture?' She dropped his hand and turned her attention back to the one thing that was real.

'Of course.' The sonographer printed out a strip of still photos and handed them to Emmy.

'I'd like one of those too.' Sam leaned in close to put in his request.

Emmy wanted to believe he was genuinely interested in his future role as a father, but she remained sceptical, unwilling to get dragged any further into this fantasy when she was the one who would end up getting hurt.

'Is everything all right with the baby?' That was the most important thing and why she resented Sam distracting her.

'All is as it should be,' she was reassured. 'So, Mum, what are your plans for the rest of the day?'

'Nothing too energetic. I think I'll put my feet up and enjoy the peace and quiet while I can.' It was going to be a major life change when she had a crying baby interrupting the usual silence in her apartment. She was looking forward to it.

Now she knew everything was all right, she could enjoy her pregnancy and look forward to the baby's arrival.

'I thought maybe we could get a cuppa somewhere and have a chat.' Sam wedged himself into the conversation and her plans for the afternoon. It was something she would have to get used to, unless she set some ground rules, or he got bored playing supportive partner. Whichever came first.

Instead of going to the noisy canteen, Sam decided to get takeaway drinks from the small coffee shop by the hospital entrance.

'Why don't we take these outside?' He wanted a little more privacy for their deeply personal conversation and thought they could get a vitamin D fix at the same time.

'It would be nice to get a break from fluorescent lights into the sunshine.'

He was grateful for Emmy's co-operation when he knew she simply wanted to go home. She had not tried to hide her exasperation at him tagging along to the scan. It was understandable for her to be defensive or suspicious of his motives when he had made it clear in the past he would not entertain the idea of having a family. Now it was happening he would do everything he could to make her believe he had their baby's interests at heart. Even if he had lost his chance with Emmy after his reckless behaviour.

They took a seat on the bench in the children's play park adjacent to the hospital. It was the perfect sunny day and, in different circumstances, they would have been sitting here celebrating, fawning over the pictures of their baby, instead of acting like strangers, sitting as far apart as they could.

'Thank you for letting me be a part of today.'

'You're the father, Sam. I'm not going to stop you but neither am I forcing you to be involved.' A guarded Emmy was not giving him an inch when it came to trusting him and he could see why. As well as his issues with his parents, Sam's reputation did not exactly scream commitment or that he was father material. His string of love interests had given her cause to tease him in the old days and now it was coming back to haunt him. The ghosts of girlfriends past had suddenly become an obstacle to the mother of his baby believing his sincerity in wanting to raise his own child.

He took a sip of his dark roast coffee, hoping the caffeine injection would also give his persuasive skills a boost. 'Have you thought any more about my proposal?'

'Yeah. You could have done it somewhere romantic like the top of the Eiffel Tower and preferably not in the presence of my family.'

Emmy continued sipping from her bottle of water, leaving Sam snorting his coffee at the comment. At least she was keeping her sense of humour, even if she no longer felt the same way about him as she once did.

'I meant about us getting married and giving the baby the best start in life.' He wasn't fooled, Emmy knew exactly what he was referring to. She was simply trying to avoid the question. Something he was no longer going to accept when they had so much to sort out over the next six months before the birth.

She sighed and leaned back in her seat, watching the children play in the park. Sam wished he could read her mind. Before fooling around in that hotel room together, she had been an open book to him. While he did not regret a single second of their time together, he longed for the closeness they once shared.

'We don't have to get married because I'm pregnant. My father and brother aren't going to come after you with a shotgun until you make me a respectable married woman.'

'I know that, but think of the benefits of us getting married. You and the baby will be financially stable, entitled to half of my assets.

Not to mention having two parents at home sharing the responsibilities.'

If they were not going to be a couple in any other sense, with Emmy hating the sight of him now, Sam thought it more provident to go down the practical route.

'You're talking about a business transaction?'

Sam saw her interest piqued and jumped on it. 'Yes. That's exactly what our marriage would be. One of convenience.'

If that was the only way he could sell it to her he was willing to sign the contract right now.

CHAPTER FIVE

EMMY WAS BEAMING as she walked onto the ward praying that the kids could not see the puffiness around her eyes from where she had been crying.

Her overactive hormones were making her more sensitive than usual, but it was Sam who had caused her latest bout of self-pity. A marriage proposal was supposed to be romantic, the special moment in a relationship to be cherished for ever. Instead, the only circumstances Sam would consider making her his wife was because she was having his baby. Love and romance did not come into it. At least, not on his part. For Sam it was merely a contract to cement his place in his child's life. A noble gesture, if it were not for the fact Emmy wanted more. There was nothing for her to gain in this arrangement, unless she counted extra heartache. That would be guaranteed, going into a marriage of convenience with a groom she had given her heart to a long time ago.

'Hey, you. How are you feeling today, Liam?' She started with her young epileptic patient who had had a rough night according to the staff at this morning's handover.

Despite his pale colour and half-closed eyes, he still managed to give her a great big smile. Emmy's heart broke for him, as it did for every child here who should have been outside enjoying their childhood.

'Tired,' he said, fighting to keep his eyes open.

'You get your rest when you can. You need it.' She pulled the curtains around his bed to give him a sense of privacy so he could sleep better. Not easy amidst the hustle and bustle of a children's hospital, with people coming and going, and the noise of the machines monitoring the well-being of those in residence.

Emmy liked to check in with each of the patients when she started her shifts to see for herself how they were doing. Plus, it was good for them to get to know her face when there were so many health professionals tending to them. Getting acquainted with her gave them some sense of security and she knew how vital that was to a child who was scared and vulnerable. The Jenningses had been her lifeline during her tumultuous childhood, and if it had not been for their steady, calm presence in her life, she might still be floundering around, in danger of drowning.

Not that everything in her life was plain sailing now, but that was as a result of her dubious adult decisions.

Her thoughts drifted to the other life she was about to bring into the world and let her hand rest on her belly, attempting to let him or her know she would do her very best to make them feel safe. That was the promise she was making above all else.

'Emmy, can I talk to you? In private?' Sam was hovering nearby, as he always seemed to be these days. Giving her no space to breathe or to think about anything other than him. At a time when she had plenty of other things to be concerned about.

He had no right to stand there looking so devastatingly handsome in his white coat, when her waistline had all but disappeared already. By the end of her third trimester she was going to be the size of a house.

Unfortunately, there was no way out but past the attractive human drape in the doorway. In another few months she would literally have to squeeze by him and that would drive her even more nuts.

'I'm working, Sam. Can't this wait until later?' She wanted some time away from the constant overthinking which resulted from their every conversation. His suggestion that they should get married for the baby's sake was something she could not get out of her head. It was a ridiculous notion which could never work, yet once upon a time she had considered that scenario as her ultimate happy-ever-after.

Whether he intended to rescind the offer of making her his wife, or wanted to try and persuade her again it was the way forward, this was not the time or place to have that discussion.

None of her colleagues knew their history and she would have preferred to keep it that way for now. Goodness knew how long Sam would stick around, so there seemed little point in making herself the subject of hospital gossip in the interim. Getting pregnant by the new consultant was not something she was keen to discuss with her colleagues. It would not do either of their reputations any favours.

'I actually wanted to talk to you about Marcus Moseley. We should probably go somewhere more private to chat.'

'Yes. Of course.' She rushed past him then, running from her own *faux pas*. Just because she was obsessed with him and her current situation did not mean he was too. They were at work, and unlike her today, he could separate their personal lives from their professional duties.

Sam placed his hand in the small of her back as they walked towards one of the empty consultation rooms. It was a small but intimate gesture, which she hoped no one else noticed. To her mind there was an element of possession there in his touch, maybe even protectiveness, and not something she imagined he would do to another colleague without consent. If any other male member of staff had put his hands on her, Emmy would have been quick to point out it was unwanted and inappropriate. In Sam's case, she knew it was instinctive because she was carrying his baby. What was more, she liked the sub-conscious gesture and the feel of him pressed against her even for a short while. It was a connection they had not made since the wedding and something she missed.

Sam had always been a very tactile person, hugging her when he visited, and she loved that warm, solid security of his body wrapped around her. His hand on her back was the most she could hope for after their last encounter had got too physical and caused all the trouble.

She was content to stand to talk but Sam pulled over a chair and insisted she sat down, whilst he leaned his body back against the desk.

'What do you know about him?' he asked.

'Same as you. Presenting with arm pain, and X-rays show past untreated fracture which hasn't healed properly. Why?'

'Do you know anything about his home life?' Sam was frowning and Emmy wondered if his thoughts had gone to the same place as hers. Something did not sit right about Marcus's story. He was a quiet boy, yet his mother acted as though he was the bane of her life. It was not the typical behaviour of a mother at the bedside of her poorly son. She was not a parent herself yet, but Emmy liked to think she would have more concern for her offspring if they were in pain to the point of being hospitalised.

'Not really. His mother always appears to be distracted, in a hurry to get back to work. I've never met the father and I don't think he has any siblings. Do you think there's something going on that social services need to know about?'

'Perhaps. I don't have proof of anything untoward. I know there were no other missed injuries picked up… Call it a hunch but something feels off.'

Emmy nodded. 'I know what you mean, and neither were able to give valid reasons for him not coming in when he first injured himself…if that's what happened.'

Sam shifted his position slightly, as though uneasy about the subject they could be dealing with. 'Do you think there's any physical abuse going on with Marcus at home?'

A shudder reverberated through Emmy's body at the thought of someone hurting their own child. It was bad enough her parents had wounded her emotionally, but it must be devastating to have someone who is supposed to love and protect you being the one inflicting pain. It happened, of course, and Emmy had dealt with domestic violence cases before. However, now she was expecting a child of her own it seemed all the more harrowing. Despite the circumstances and timing of her pregnancy, she had nothing but love for her little one already.

Her hand went protectively to her belly, her eyes filling with tears for those babies who were not as lucky as this one who had a mother who would do anything to protect it.

'I didn't see any other unusual activity on his file.' She had made a point of checking in case there was any evidence of historic abuse which they might have missed.

'Well, given that he wasn't brought in for treatment with this last broken bone, I don't think we can rely on his records being an accurate depiction of his medical background.'

'You're right. I guess I was just praying that my own suspicions weren't justified.' Her eyes were burning with the threat of tears, and though she fought making a scene, Sam was already moving towards her.

'Hey. I know this is a tough one. If you

want, I can take it from here?' He was holding both of her hands in his, doing his best to reassure her everything was going to be okay.

Emmy would have given anything for one of his hugs in that moment, but she knew it would be inappropriate on so many levels. Instead, she sniffed away the tears and straightened her back.

'No. I want to probe a bit deeper and see what's going on for myself. I still have a duty of care to the patients here.' It was not going to be easy but her emotions should not interfere with her work.

There was a way to go before the baby arrived, months of being emotional and dealing with sick children, but she could not turn her back simply because it was upsetting. Those children, her patients, needed her. Being a good mother was all about putting her child first and she saw her job at the hospital as good training. Her birth parents had not stuck by her when things got tough and that made her all the more determined to stay strong for others. Dealing with vulnerable children was part of her job and her conscience would not let her back away simply because it was a difficult situation. Children like Marcus needed people like her and Sam who were willing to go the extra mile for their patients. 'That's all well and good, Emmy, but I don't want you stressing yourself out unnecessarily.'

If she believed Sam's concern was for her she might have found it endearing, but she was sure he was thinking only of his baby. Yes, that was a good thing that he cared at all when she had expected him to run as soon as he found out he was going to be a dad. However, she was more than just an incubator for his offspring, and she was not going to be dictated to or lose her identity simply because she was becoming a mother. They were not together, so he had no say over anything she did.

'I may be pregnant, but I'm still capable of doing my job. It's going to be a long six months if you scrutinise my every move for the duration. The baby is yours but I'm not.' And that was the crux of the problem and her outburst. She wanted to be his, longed for that protective side of Sam's to be for her. It wasn't jealousy—goodness knew she was happy her baby had two parents who adored it—but for the rest of her life she was going to be on the outside of Sam's deepest affections, and that hurt. With her history, she should have been used to that feeling, but it never got any easier.

She attempted a dramatic flounce out of the room but could not see the handle clearly through her blurred vision.

'Hey,' Sam said softly, and closed his hand over hers. 'I'm only looking out for you. I don't mean to come across as domineering. Of course you do whatever you're happy with. All I'm saying is I'm here to share the load with you.'

That was what was making everything so much harder for Emmy. If he had washed his hands of her and the baby and disappeared out of their lives for good, she would not have to see him every day, or be reminded that he did not want her. In time she might even have got over him. Impossible now when he was part of her life, showing her every day what a good man he was deep down. It was not Sam's fault he did not feel for her what she had always felt for him.

Emmy sighed. Pushing him away was not going to do anyone any good.

'Why don't you have a chat with Marcus, and I'll see if I can get any information from the mother? I don't want to take things any further unless we have to or unless there is any proof he is being deliberately hurt.'

'If you're sure—' Sam's tone and the look of concern were indication he did not think it was a good idea, but she thought it made sense for them to continue their investigation separately. Not to mention safer for her peace of mind.

It only took one glare for him to hold his hands up. 'Okay, okay. You know best.' He was smirking at her now and that was not any easier to deal with than the pity eyes.

Unless she poked her own eyeballs out, or wore a blindfold around him, she was going to be in trouble for a long time to come.

Emmy's palms were sweating, her heart galloping, and Sam was not anywhere in sight for her to blame it all on. It was seeing Mrs Moseley coming down the corridor which had her in a tizz. Confronting a parent with such a serious accusation was going to be tough and she had no way of knowing how the woman would react. She wondered if Sam was right and she was putting herself and the baby in harm's way if she chose to lash out.

Unfortunately, violent outbursts towards staff were commonplace these days and it was more than her pride at stake today. Except, if Emmy decided to make things official at this stage, before she knew the facts, she could be making things worse for the boy. She did not want to see him taken into care on her say-so; she would never forgive herself if she got things wrong.

She would have an informal chat, more of a fact-finding mission than pointing an accusing finger straight away. According to Sam, Marcus had closed up when he had tried talking to him, giving nothing away, so this was their last attempt to get to the truth before they would be forced to go to the authorities.

'Mrs Moseley, I wondered if I could have a word with you in here?' Emmy opened the door to the family room in an attempt to herd her inside.

'I suppose...' Although she looked wary, she let Emmy lead her into the room. 'Is Marcus all right?'

She did not sit in any of the armchairs provided for the comfort of the families visiting seriously ill relatives, clearly worried about the reason behind being sequestered into a side room.

Emmy took a seat and gestured for her to do the same, the reassuring smile she was projecting covering her own anxiety caused by the situation.

'Yes, he's fine. I just wanted to have a chat with you about anything which might be going on at home.' Emmy tried to keep her tone light and casual to avoid any unpleasantness but was aware that she was encroaching on the woman's private life.

'There's nothing going on at home that concerns you.' Any conviviality evaporated with the thinning of Mrs Moseley's lips and defensive folding of her arms.

Emmy sat forward in her chair in an attempt to close the distance between them. 'I'm not here to judge you. My job is to make Marcus better and sometimes things at home can impact on a child's health.'

'What exactly are you accusing me of?' Narrowing eyes matched the thin lips.

Emmy swallowed hard, feeling as though she was the one under scrutiny here. 'I'm not accusing you of anything, Mrs Moseley. There are just a few things we're concerned about and hoped you could clarify some matters for us. I…we…wondered how a fracture like that could have been missed for so long. Marcus must have been in pain at the time. Is there a reason you didn't bring him into hospital before now?'

Silence.

Emmy tried again. 'I'm trying to help you but if I suspect Marcus is being physically harmed, I have a duty to report it. So far, you're giving me nothing to dissuade me of that notion.' There was part of Emmy wishing she had allowed Sam to be involved in this with her so he could have been the one playing bad cop. Not that he would have been convincing as anything other than a concerned member of staff either, but she could have used the backup.

Sam was good at giving her a boost and support when he thought she needed it. Emmy was sure she was on the verge of hitting a nerve or being on the receiving end of a right hook for questioning another woman's parenting.

Mrs Moseley suddenly burst into tears, leaving Emmy scrabbling to find the box of tissues usually kept here for such emotionally charged occasions. It turned out she was correct in her assumption, just not in the way she had expected.

'I didn't hurt him, despite what you think,' Marcus's mother sniffed in between sobs.

As Emmy passed over the hankies, she could see now how tired the woman looked close up with unwashed hair, bags under her eyes and no attempt to cover them with make-up. This outburst was a sign she had reached her emotional limit.

'Take all the time you need,' Emmy coached, softly, encouraging her to continue with her story. She knew better than anyone how cathartic it was to share one's worries. Despite how the news of her pregnancy had come to light, and Sam's chivalrous but mis-judged proposal, it was a weight off her mind not having to keep the secret any longer.

Mrs Moseley dabbed at her eyes with the tissue and sniffed back further tears. 'Sorry. It hasn't been easy.'

Without any further information Emmy could not be sure if she was talking about parenting in general or if there was a more sinister context. She had to push for more.

'With Marcus?'

The woman nodded and Emmy's heart sank into her comfortable shoes. Was this confirmation that the child had borne the brunt of his mother's frustrations with him? She hoped not. The emotionally charged silence seemed to stretch for ever before Mrs Moseley cleared her throat to speak again.

'He's not a bad child…just difficult to manage sometimes.'

'And you…you discipline him when he acts out?' It was the logical conclusion for Emmy to come to, if not the most palatable one.

'No! I told you, I would never hurt him, but I can't watch him twenty-four hours a day.'

'He hurt himself?' Though it came as something of a relief, it still did not explain why the mother had not sought adequate treatment for her son at the time of injury.

She nodded. 'He's always getting into scrapes but I have two jobs. I can't take time off every time he falls over or gets into mischief.'

'Isn't there someone who can help out? Family or friends?'

She gave an emphatic 'No.'

'Is his father around?' Normally, Emmy would not pry into people's personal lives but she was trying to ascertain what sort of support system was in place for the family, if any.

'Only when it suits him. That doesn't stop him from threatening to take custody of Marcus though, just to spite me. He's no father to Marcus, but if he thought he could use an accident against me, he would.'

'That's why you didn't bring Marcus in earlier?'

'I didn't realise he'd actually broken the bone or I swear I would have brought him before now. He seemed fine after a day or two, so I thought he'd pulled a muscle or something. You've got to understand, my ex-husband walked out and left us with nothing. I'm working two jobs just to make ends meet. I know the break-up has affected Marcus too, and with me working so much, he's been playing up for attention. I'm run ragged. Being a parent isn't easy.' The tears began to fall again in earnest and Emmy reached out a hand to comfort her, her own eyes welling up in sympathy. She could very well find herself in the same situation at some point: overworked, overtired, guilty about leaving a child at home and struggling to find adequate childcare, as well as managing to pay all of the bills. At least Sam wanted to be in the picture. Emotions aside, having him involved could make a big difference to her on the practical side.

His business proposal to get married was beginning to make sense now she could see where things could lead if she insisted on doing everything herself. Mrs Moseley didn't have a choice, but she did.

Sam was offering a partnership, sharing time and financial responsibilities so they could give their baby the best start in life. It was selfish to turn that down for the sake of her own pride. She was sure Mrs Moseley would have jumped at the chance if an attractive, successful man had given her the same deal. Okay, so love was not part of the contract but that did not pay the bills or give a person peace of mind. This woman and her son were deeply unhappy and that was not a future Emmy wanted for herself and her child.

'Listen, I'll go and get you a cup of tea and you can take a few minutes to compose yourself. If it's all right with you, I'd like to make a few calls and see if I can get you some help.'

'I don't want social services to think I'm

not coping.' There was panic in her eyes, along with the determination to carry on regardless of the cost to her emotionally and physically. Emmy knew she would be the same if there was a threat of someone trying to take her child away hanging over her. It was about time someone gave her a break.

'Social services will have to get involved, but I do want to see if there is any other help available to you. Perhaps there's a charitable organisation with after-school clubs. Somewhere for Marcus to go and run off some of his excess energy and meet new friends. I'll see what I can do.'

'Thank you.'

By the time Emmy left the room Mrs Moseley was smiling again and looking years younger at the prospect of getting some help.

Emmy's new task was hitting close to home. She had dealt with single-parent groups in the past in relation to her patients and their families, but this time was different. She knew she could be availing of their services herself in time, depending on how well she managed to juggle work, childcare and the cost of raising a child on her own. There was one person who could save her from that uncertain future. At least Sam wanted to be a dad, to contribute to his baby's upbringing. If only she could learn to live with her husband not loving her, marriage could be the perfect solution to avoiding a similar situation to Mrs Moseley.

CHAPTER SIX

As soon as Sam was finished with his patients, he went in search of Emmy. His attempt to get some information from Marcus
had proved fruitless and he had spent most
of the afternoon worried about how Emmy's
chat with the mother had gone. He had always been protective towards her but now she
was carrying his baby he wanted to wrap her
up and keep them both safe from the outside
world. Although she had made it pretty clear
that was not an option available to him.

Emmy had always been headstrong and independent, qualities he admired but which
were now driving him crazy. It was those
helping her to push him away, Emmy believing him too unreliable to be a father or a husband. He was a chip off the old block after all.
Regardless of the vow he had made never to
get into this situation, he still believed himself

to be a better human being than his father. Something he was now having to take a second look at. He did not blame Emmy for not trusting him, but he wanted to give her reason to start. Proposing marriage had been his way of showing her that commitment. She knew he had never wanted to be tied down, but he was willing to do that for her and the baby. Even if the marriage would be in name only.

It was a big undertaking on his part and after his chat with Marcus he was more aware of that than ever. Having a child was a huge responsibility, fraught with all kinds of worry and sacrifice. Only time would tell if he was up to the job or if Emmy would even let him try.

He saw her emerge from one of the cubicles and the tension ebbed from his bones to see she was physically unharmed after her confrontation with Mrs Moseley.

'Emmy! Did everything go all right with Marcus's mother?'

'Yes. She was very emotional and apologetic. Nothing sinister, but she is struggling. It appears Marcus's father has left, and things are acrimonious between the couple.'

It was a relief to discover Marcus was not

in any immediate danger at home. Sam did not like having families split up if it was preventable. Yet there was something about the tale which made him uneasy on a more personal level. Another family had been torn apart and left bleeding, the mother the one dealing with the fallout, and the son suffering as a result. The children were never to blame for their parents' actions but always the ones impacted most. It was Sam's worst fear to cause such pain to others, but he might not get much say in what happened.

If Emmy continued to keep him at arm's length, would he ever be involved in his child's life at all? He did not relish the idea of being kept out of the picture. It would still leave Emmy to do the majority of the parenting and deal with all the highs and lows which came with it.

'Is there anything we can do to help?'

'I've contacted social services and put her in touch with a few local groups who support single-parent families. Hopefully Marcus can get back to being a kid again and forget everything going on with his parents.'

'I'm sure they'll appreciate that. The whole matter is making me re-evaluate our situation too, Emmy. Perhaps we should get something in writing about custody arrangements.'

'Isn't that a tad premature? The baby isn't here yet, but when it is, your name will be on the birth certificate.'

Although that was reassuring, Sam was concerned in case any future bad feeling would affect that and leave him without any parental rights.

'It's not that I don't trust you, Emmy, but we know family matters can get complicated. We should seek some legal advice on the subject just in case.'

She frowned at the idea. 'Do you really think that's necessary, Sam? We've known each other for practically our whole lives. This is a baby, not a car or a house you can just claim ownership over.'

'What else do you suggest? How are we going to move forward, both of us confident and secure about where we stand?' Naturally they both had reservations when this was not the ideal basis for bringing a new life into the world. If he had been sensible and done things properly, he would have wooed Emmy, given her reason to trust him and maybe even love him. Ideally they would have been in a proper relationship before even thinking about starting a family but now it was about damage control.

'Dealing with Marcus has made me think about things too. It's made me see the practical benefits of having two parents working together instead of each pretending the other doesn't exist. If the offer is still there on the table to be your wife, I'd like to close the deal.'

The sudden turnaround left Sam's head spinning. He had been hoping to at least get paternity rights down on paper but now it seemed as though Emmy was prepared to give him so much more.

'Are you saying—?'

'Yes, Sam. If the offer is still there, I'd like to marry you. That should give us both some security over the arrangements, shouldn't it?' Emmy was smiling but there was a brightness missing from her eyes to convince him she was truly on board with the decision.

This should have been the happiest moment of their lives, entering into a lifelong commitment to one another. Instead, he knew it was more out of necessity, a convenient way of sharing responsibility for their mistake. As if getting someone pregnant and having to marry had ever been on his agenda. Sam knew he had already ruined Emmy's life and all he could do was try to make amends now she thought there was no better future for her than to marry someone she did not love.

'I think we should do it as soon as possible.' Before either of them changed their minds. It was not the most romantic engagement but if this was purely a business transaction, there should be no misunderstanding. No one would get fooled into thinking this was a real relationship or run the risk of anyone getting hurt. Then he could stop fretting over why she did not truly want him.

Sam faced himself in the mirror as he pinned the white carnation to his buttonhole. Something perhaps his best man or mother should have done for him on his wedding day, but he had neither. This was not a conventional marriage after all.

It was going to appear odd to the outside world who were unaware of his arrangement with Emmy that there would be no traditional 'groom's side' but it did not seem right in the circumstances. Not least because he had minimal contact with his mother. Having her present simply for appearances' sake would not have made the day any easier. He was already a bag of nerves at the prospect of marrying Emmy without the added worry of his mother's presence. Seeing her there— a bitter, broken woman who was the result of his father's behaviour—would only impress on him the importance of not messing up the marriage or being a father. He was under enough pressure to make things work since he had talked Emmy into this crazy scheme.

Strangely, getting ready today felt very much like preparing for the real thing. He was nervous about getting the vows right and making this commitment. In putting himself forward as a suitable husband to Emmy, he was saying he would be there for her and the baby. That she could rely on him. In reality, he was praying that to be true when he had no practical experience of being a husband or a father. Roles he thought he would never have to prepare for, yet now he was taking on both, he would admit to some sense of excitement along with the anxiety.

A future with Emmy was not something

completely abhorrent to him or he would never have proposed it. In fact, he was looking forward to having more than snatched moments with her without interruption from her family. A big part of him was secretly hoping they might develop a relationship beyond the façade when their partnership was so good in all other areas.

They were going to be spending a lot of time together for the foreseeable future, raising the child Sam never thought he would have. Now that fatherhood was a certainty there were aspects of that which appealed to him too. A chance to create the family neither he nor Emmy had been afforded growing up. Pride in his child's achievements, being there for every milestone no matter how small and enjoying days out at the seaside or the zoo were all simple things he had been denied by his father but were things he was now looking forward to participating in.

As Sam pondered the happy occasions soon available to him if he chose to embrace his new path as a husband and father, today did not seem as frightening as it once had. Hopefully his future wife would come to the same conclusion.

* * *

'Are you ready to do this?' Sam was standing at the open car door smiling and waiting for Emmy to take his arm.

She said, 'Yes,' when really, she wanted to scream, 'No, not like this!'

From here on in, she doubted she would ever say what she was really thinking or feeling to Sam. It was not in the contract.

Today she was going to become Mrs Goodwin. In name at least. It had been a whirlwind few weeks since they had managed to secure a spot at the register office. Neither had wanted a big wedding, not when this was nothing more than an arrangement between them. It meant keeping it a secret from her family, who would have insisted on the whole extravagance of a white church wedding, and all the expense and headaches which came with it. It did not seem fair or necessary when they weren't some loved-up couple having the day of their lives.

Now, however, walking up the steps to the town hall, she wondered if they had done the right thing in keeping it quiet. The family would be so disappointed to have missed out, and if she was honest, she was a little emotional that they were not here for her wedding day, even if it was just for show.

'Well, don't you scrub up well, sis? Going somewhere?'

When David stepped out into the marble hallway to greet them, Emmy nearly passed out from shock.

'David? What are you doing here?'

'Did you really think I was going to let my little sister and best friend get married without me?'

Emmy let go of Sam's arm and threw herself at David, so pleased to have his support on a day when she knew her nerves would be tested to the limit.

Sam cleared his throat. 'I know we agreed to keep things low key, but I couldn't let you go through this without your family.'

It was then she noticed the others hovering nearby, clearly worried about being unwanted.

'I'm so glad you all came.' She transferred her affections to her parents, hugging them hard, and even stopped for a brief embrace with the twins.

'We don't want to intrude if you'd rather we weren't here,' her father mumbled, and

Emmy immediately wished she had included them from the start.

'Of course I want you here. We just didn't want a big fuss. I would love for you to give me away, Dad.' At least that part would be genuine and filled with real emotion even if the rest of the ceremony was not.

'You look so beautiful.' Her mother was already dabbing her eyes with a handkerchief and Emmy was glad she had loved ones here supporting her, rather than some stranger they had roped in to witness proceedings.

'Thank you.' In keeping with the low-key nature of the day, she had avoided a big flouncy gown in favour of a white lace shift dress and some flowers in her hair. Sam had presented her with a posy of wildflowers he had picked himself that morning as a bouquet to add to her Bohemian look and she loved it.

He was the perfect, handsome groom in his navy three-piece suit and her family had come dressed for the occasion in outfits she knew had been bought specially for the last-minute occasion. If anyone had any misgivings about the venue or the timing, they had the decency not to say anything for now. Emmy was appreciative when the doubts had been creeping in over these past days anyway.

She had moved her belongings into Sam's house the previous weekend, setting up in a separate bedroom to his, of course. Not how most women began their married life, but this was what she had agreed to—a loveless arrangement. Who would not have had second thoughts about that? But here she was, ready to do it, and now her family were here there was no going back.

'Are we ready to go through?' The registrar ushered them into the small side room, the guests barely taking up the front row of seats.

Despite the informality, her father walked her down the short aisle and very seriously answered, 'I do,' when asked who was giving Emmy away.

At that moment, she had a sudden urge to cling to him all the tighter, when he had been her source of stability for so long. Now she was being handed over to Sam, she was trusting him to do as good a job.

He looked as anxious as she felt when they met at the end of the aisle and she realised the enormity of this to him too. A man who had always said marriage and babies were not for him was marrying her simply out of a sense of duty. This was not a fairy-tale ending for him either. Judging by his pallid colour, it was more like the stuff of nightmares.

They said the traditional vows as they exchanged plain gold bands, though Emmy's voice had trembled as she did so. She almost broke completely when saying, 'I do.'

This was not how marriage was supposed to be and, looking into Sam's eyes, she could see her own sadness reflected in them.

They were both trapped, making the best of a bad situation. The worst of it was her family watching, believing this was real and that they had found love together. If only.

'You may kiss the bride.' The registrar confirmed they were now husband and wife before dropping that surprise on them.

'Is that really a thing? We don't have to,' she whispered to her groom.

'We may as well give the people what they want,' he replied with a grin before moving in for their first kiss as a married couple.

She was poised, ready for a peck on the lips to satisfy her family they were together for all the right reasons. What she got was hot enough to make her forget this was fake.

Somewhere in the distance she heard David cheering and her father discreetly coughing. Her sisters were likely sniggering somewhere too, but she did not care because Sam's lips were on hers again for the first time in months.

There was still that same urgency that she remembered in his kiss, as though he had been starved of her for too long. Exactly how she felt about him.

He had to spoil the illusion when he broke away and winked at her. 'That should do the trick.'

Emmy had to hand it to him, he was a very good actor. For a moment he had fooled her into thinking he was actually sealing their future together with a heartfelt kiss. Every time she was in danger of getting caught up in the supposed romance, Sam was there bringing her back down to earth and reminding her that he personally was not part of the deal.

It took a lot of effort to force her trembling mouth into a smile when she turned to face her family.

'Congratulations!'

Every good wish and kiss on the cheek brought Emmy closer to tears. Confetti rained on her like the colourful, tattered remnants of her romantic hopes and dreams. Sam stopped at the top of the steps and turned her face to his. There was no hiding her pain from him now.

'Hey,' he said softly, tilting her chin up. 'It's over now.'

He dropped a quick kiss on her mouth, grounding her and reassuring her he was there with her.

That was when she heard the click of a camera and began to question the real motive behind the kiss. Would she ever believe anything he said again if she was always convinced it was only for appearances' sake?

Sam might think the worst was over, but Emmy was worried it was just the beginning.

'A toast to the happy couple.'

Mr Jennings raised his glass and encouraged the others to do the same. He received a muted response, but they could not expect a rapturous celebration with only half a dozen guests present. They fitted into one corner of the local bar they had gone to for the impromptu wedding reception.

Sam knew every second was killing Emmy

inside and his fake smile was making his jaw ache. This was not what they had planned for their wedding day in any shape or form but at the last minute he had decided Emmy should have her family around her.

A decision he was sure she appreciated and which also meant he would keep on Dave's good side. What he had not counted on was the day carrying on after the ceremony and signing of the register. Poor Emmy could not even drink to get her through the enforced reception.

She deserved so much more than she was getting today but she had not wanted a whole palaver and he understood why. There was not a whole lot to celebrate, at least not in the traditional sense. This wasn't an occasion to mark the start of their new life together, it signified the end of their independent lives. From here on in they were together for selfless reasons, not because they could not imagine an existence without one another. He would go as far as to say, given the choice, Emmy could live without ever seeing him again. One night and he had destroyed the future she might have envisioned for herself.

Whatever she thought of him she could not hate him any more than he hated himself.

'So, when are you going on honeymoon? I guess with the money you saved on feeding guests and a band, you have something amazing planned?' Lisa had that smug look on her face she always wore when she stirred up trouble. Sam did not know how Emmy had endured the endless mocking for so long without slapping it off her face.

He supposed it came from a lifetime of listening to the constant digs and put-downs which had somehow become acceptable to the family. Even now she had her head bowed taking everything that was being thrown at her in that subservient pose. The others excused or ignored the twins' behaviour and Sam knew he was guilty of that too. Now she was his wife he was entitled to defend her if he deemed it necessary.

On this occasion he realised he was at fault for not organising something, or at least coming up with a reason for not booking a trip away to throw everyone off the scent of their arranged marriage.

'I...er...' Mr and Mrs Jennings were waiting to hear their exciting plans and Dave was listening intently too. How was Sam going to explain away not giving his little sister the trip of her dreams without getting a good pasting?

'With work, and the pregnancy, we thought we'd wait. We'll make it a family holiday when the baby arrives. Right, hon?' Emmy batted her eyelashes and linked her arm through his as she got him off the hook.

'Right. We'll have plenty of time for holidays. For now, we're content simply spending time with each other.' He patted her hand with the sickly sweet sentiment, knowing it could not be further from the truth. They had nothing planned beyond the legal ceremony but there would be expectations from everyone else. Things had happened so fast they had not really thought things through properly. Going back to work would be fun trying to explain. As far as anyone there knew they had only met, and this would seem like a whirlwind romance. Not a lifelong bond which had somehow morphed into a marriage of inconvenience for both of them.

Emmy stamped on his foot under the table, a reminder not to overdo it. Dave was already eyeing them with some suspicion. Maybe if Sam got them drunk they would forget how strange this all was.

CHAPTER SEVEN

EMMY'S WEDDING NIGHT turned out to be anticlimactic on so many levels. There was no romantic getaway to look forward to, far from work, family and any other stresses. Perhaps she should have booked herself a solo trip somewhere and put some distance between her and Sam one last time before they entered into their forced proximity.

As it was, they were heading home together, alone, to start their new life of domestic indifference. They walked through the door of his house and she wondered if they were supposed to go their separate ways and do their own thing now that the show was over.

'I wanted to say thank you again for inviting my family. I appreciate it made things more difficult in some ways but I'm glad they were there.' Emmy kicked off her shoes in the hall and popped her posy of flowers into a vase on the side table.

'No problem. I'm sorry I couldn't give you the day you deserved but I thought having them there would help.' Sam hung up his jacket and it seemed absurd to be returning to the mundane, still dressed in their wedding finery.

'It did but I have to say I was relieved when we finally poured them into taxis.' Emmy had sat with her soft drinks watching the others celebrate their nuptials with copious amounts of alcohol. Sam hadn't indulged as much as her family but did not take the risk of driving anyway. Their wedding dinner had consisted of pub snacks and crisps but she had been the one against a grand 'do.' It would have weighed even heavier on her conscience if they had paid a fortune for the ruse.

Yet, she had a feeling Sam would have given her anything she had asked for to make her happy. He was trying to make this bearable but only time would tell how long that would last. He might come to resent the commitment he had made in the heat of the moment. Especially if he went on to meet someone else.

The thought of him bringing another woman home with him made her sick but her claim to him was in name only. That was part of the marriage they had not discussed. It was all very well entering into a convenient partnership but she could not expect him to remain celibate.

They turned to each other in a 'What now?' moment now the hard part was over. Emmy's thoughts slipped back to the kiss they had shared during the ceremony and she would have been happy to carry on from where they had left off. They both had needs and she would not be averse to maintaining the physical aspect of the marriage. It might prevent Sam from seeking sexual gratification elsewhere and provide her with some of the intimacy she craved with him. Even if the relationship still lacked the emotional side of a relationship.

'I guess I'll be heading to bed. It's been a long day.' It appeared Sam, however, had had enough already. That did not bode well for a long-lasting marriage if he was desperate to get away from her on what was supposed to be their wedding night.

'Oh. Okay.'

'Unless you had something else in mind? Feel free to watch the TV in the lounge and make yourself a cup of tea. Maybe you would like a bath? This is your house now too so you're welcome to do as you please.' Regardless of his generosity, Sam was giving her the warmth of a bed-and-breakfast owner letting her use a room for the night.

'I'm sure I can find something to amuse myself. Thanks.' What Emmy wanted now was to strip off this layer of pretence and wash away all traces of the day. Thankfully, she had a shower in her en suite bathroom to do that without fear of running into Sam. He might have just married the mother of his child but she wondered if they would see much of each other at all.

'Goodnight, then, Emmy.' He gave her a swift peck on the cheek.

Her eyes fluttered shut, replaying the kiss he had given her earlier in front of their audience. She supposed he did not have anyone to convince any more and this was as good as it was getting.

'Night.'

She waited for him to retire to his room first, thinking it too tragic for them to split off into their separate rooms at the same time on their wedding night. Her breath hitched in her throat when she heard the door slam, sounding the death knell on her love life for good.

Sam had barely slept. How could he, hearing his new wife cry herself to sleep in the next room? As a result he had been up since dawn in an attempt to make amends for the disappointment he had caused her.

Although the marriage was not a conventional one, he should have made more of an effort. Emmy still needed, and deserved, to be treated like a cherished wife. He had made the mistake of thinking she would want her space but Emmy had been through too much to be taken for granted and he should not have expected her to resume life as though nothing had happened. A wedding day was a big deal to anyone and he was lucky she had agreed to marry him at all after everything. If he was going to hang on to her he had to remember his life was about looking after more than number one now.

He let himself in through the front door and heard her moving about upstairs. This was the first day of the rest of their lives together and he was starting as he meant to go on. This morning, he was hoping to put a smile back on her face with breakfast.

She wandered into the kitchen, looking weary and beautiful, before he had time to plate anything up for her. He was standing at the breakfast bar and she pulled up a chair to watch him.

'Morning, Mrs Goodwin. I was going to bring this to you in bed.'

Her smile turned into a yawn. 'Sorry. I didn't sleep very well.'

His heart lurched, as he replayed the sound of her sobs in his head. 'Nor me. We should have both come downstairs and made some hot cocoa.'

Okay, so that would not have been an earth-shattering wedding night either but at least they could have been miserable in company. He hated to think of her crying in her room, believing she was alone, when they had gone into this together.

'It was a strange day for both of us.' Emmy was being generous to include him when this had affected her so much more. He longed to have her back to the carefree young woman she had been before he had screwed everything up.

'Hopefully things will settle into some sort of normalcy for us soon. Starting with breakfast.' Sam pushed the takeaway cups and bag of warm pastries towards her. She took the lid off one cup and inhaled a deep breath.

'Mmm… Coffee?'

'Decaf.' He knew how much she loved her coffee but had sacrificed it for the baby. He figured one cup of decaffeinated brew was allowed now and then if it made her happy.

'And a *pain au chocolat*?' She opened the bag and helped herself to one of the flaky pastries. 'You're spoiling me.'

Sam was glad to see her enjoying the breakfast but something so simple should not be such a special thing to her. It proved how infrequently anyone did something nice for her. It made him more convinced that he had done the right thing with the surprise he had in store for her next. It was about time someone treated her with the kindness she doled out to everyone else. As her husband, it was his job now to show her she was appreciated.

He produced the folded computer printout

from his back pocket and placed it on the counter.

'What's this?' she asked, after finishing her first bite of breakfast.

There was a small spot of melted chocolate clinging to her bottom lip and Sam had the urge to lick it off. His body was wide awake now as memories of that kiss yesterday came to mind. Again, he had got carried away and was lucky she had not slapped him in front of their wedding guests. Thankfully, he had managed to convince her it was a show he had put on to further the lie, rather than his libido beginning to rage out of control again. This torture of seeing her being so close and not being able to do anything about it was his punishment for his self-centred behaviour to date. He was going to have to learn to live with it and keep his urges at bay or run the risk of losing his wife and child in one more wrong move.

'Let's call it a wedding present.' Or a belated apology, he thought, after treating her feelings as an afterthought amongst all the wedding shenanigans.

He watched her scan the page, her eyes

widening and her hand moving towards her mouth as she gasped. 'Paris?'

'I know you always wanted to go, and we have a few days off work. I thought a mini-break might do us the world of good.'

'Yes, but... I'm not ready to go. The flight is this afternoon.'

'You look good to me.' Make-up free, with bedhead and wearing a royal blue silk chemise, Emmy was gorgeous.

If they had been a real married couple he would have taken her back to bed and happily spent the weekend there.

'That's sweet of you to lie but I really need to go shower and pack.' She bounced up out of her chair, full of energy and looking more like the old Emmy.

Her bare feet squeaked on the tiled floor as she did a one-hundred-and-eighty-degree turn and came running back towards him. Leaning over the counter, she planted a kiss on his cheek with a 'Mwah! Thank you, Sam, for everything.'

Then she took another bite of her pastry and skipped off. Sam had been up since the early hours of the morning trying to come up with something to make her smile and he had succeeded. In a flash of inspiration as the birds began to chirp their dawn chorus, he had remembered a conversation they had had a long time ago. One where they had talked about their hopes and dreams, at an age where anything seemed possible without real-life obstacles ever getting in the way.

Back then he was sure his had revolved around money, flash cars and beautiful women. All of which he had had in the past and none of which had ever made him truly content.

Emmy's aspirations had been simpler and more palatable than his materialistic wants. A good job, a family of her own and a visit to Paris. As one of life's true romantics, Emmy's current situation was all the more tragic.

Obsessed with those slushy movies where the couple always got their happy-ever-after, she had told him of her Paris dream. The city of love in her childhood fantasies was the ultimate destination. She had probably imagined her engagement beginning with a proposal atop the Eiffel Tower and a wedding to outshine those she had sobbed over in the movies.

Instead, all he had given her was a shotgun

ceremony at a register office and a staycation. Sam would never make the romantic lead in her dreams, but he could give her the best holiday possible. Maybe then she could begin to forgive him for getting them into this mess.

'Oh, Sam. It's stunning.'

The view from the hotel was something Emmy thought only existed in the movies. They were opposite the Eiffel Tower, the bustling city traffic directly below their balcony, and she could not have been happier.

She had woken up this morning resigned to her new life with Sam, which, after last night, she thought meant living separate lives. He had apparently found it a depressing enough future too, to have splurged on this extravagant venture.

Never mind the cost of the last-minute flights, he had also booked the honeymoon suite in this bijou hotel in its prime location.

'I'm so glad you like it.' He carried their luggage into the room after refusing to let her lift anything heavier than her handbag.

She took a glance around the spacious room and marvelled at the sweet vintage furniture and the soft blue-and-white floral decor. There was even a trail of rose petals leading from the claw-foot bathtub to the four-poster bed. She did a double take. One bed.

Sam must have been thinking along the same lines. 'Don't worry, I can take the sofa. I just thought you deserved something magical and this was the nicest room they had available.'

'I'm sure we can sort the sleeping arrangements out later. We are both adults.' Married ones, at that. Sharing a bed at this stage—married and expecting a baby—should not have been a problem but it was in this instance. It likely always would be for her but Emmy had agreed to this life so she would simply have to get used to it. Sam had gone to a lot of trouble to make this part of her dream come true at least.

'This is your trip so what would you like to do first?'

There were so many landmarks—l'Arc de Triomphe, the Louvre, the Eiffel Tower—to name a few. All of which she had imagined visiting with Sam at her side in her wildest dreams. Somehow this was not quite the same, but she would make the most of the situation.

'The nearest restaurant. Baby's hungry and so am I. If I can't partake in the glorious wines and cheeses available, I'm going to sample the finest cuisine this country has to offer.'

'You won't get an argument from me on that score. We can unpack later.'

Emmy supposed that was the most action this room would see tonight. Sam had covered all the romantic clichés with this surprise, except the most crucial one. Him. Still, she was lucky he had gone to so much trouble on her behalf and she would not be ungrateful. He was doing everything within his power to make her happy. At this moment in time he had succeeded.

'Have a lovely evening, Mr and Mrs Goodwin.' The receptionist beamed at them as they left the hotel.

Despite the rocky start and the unconventional arrangements, being called Mrs Goodwin did give her a buzz of satisfaction. As far as the outside world knew, Sam was hers and vice versa. Walking out into the bustling Parisian streets, they were simply another newlywed couple on honeymoon. Only she and Sam knew the truth.

'Hey, watch out!'

Before Emmy knew what was happening, Sam grabbed her hand and pulled her away from the edge of the footpath. Just in time, as someone on an electric scooter zoomed by, too close for comfort.

Sam switched places so she was on the inside, and he was walking closer to the traffic, though he did not let go of her hand. It felt right, natural, and so good to have him want to protect her.

Walking hand in hand with her new husband in Paris was everything she could have asked for as they passed the aromatic *boulangeries* and *chocolatiers*.

'You know I'm making a note of these places to revisit before we go home.'

'I don't doubt it. That's why I paid for extra baggage allowance.' Sam laughed, but unlike some family members, she knew it was not his way to make fun of her weight. That had never been an issue to him, and he had always accepted her for who she was. He might not be madly in love with her, but Emmy knew he was fond of her. Comfortable enough to let people think they were a couple without embarrassment. She had the urge to hug him close but settled for leaning her head on his shoulder. When he kissed the top of her head she almost cried with happiness, or despair. The two were so inextricably linked now it was difficult to tell. He was doing and saying all the right things, but no amount of good intentions could make any of this real.

'Why don't we stop here for a bite to eat? There's a good view of everything going on and we'll catch the last of the sun on the terrace.' Sam spied a chic bistro on the corner, the tables outside packed with chatty diners, whose various accents represented how cosmopolitan the area had become. He insisted on seating her as far away from any smokers as possible as he pulled out a chair for her.

'Such a gentleman,' she teased, only for his 'Not always' to knock her completely off her feet.

It was comments such as that and his rakish grin which made her wonder if he would be interested in a replay of what happened during her brother's evening reception or if it was simply his flirty nature. The idea of having him in her bed again sent delectable quivers of arousal whispering across her skin but the physical act could never replace the emotion, the feelings, she longed for him to have towards her.

Thankfully the waiter's arrival interrupted Emmy's yearning so she could live in the moment and enjoy the surroundings instead of moping over things Sam could not give her.

He ordered a cassoulet between them, with some fresh bread and two glasses of mineral water, impressing her with his perfect French as he did so.

'You don't have to forego the alcohol because of me,' she told him, encouraging him to enjoy one passion. It was a shame to deny him the opportunity to taste some of the finest wines in the world on her account.

'It's fine. I don't need to be drunk to enjoy myself when I'm here with you.' The warmth of his smile was a clear sign of his sincerity and helped her believe he was getting something out of this trip too.

She had been so focused on what she had lost by entering into a fake marriage with him that she never stopped to think about what Sam was feeling about it all. He was giving up more than alcohol for her and the baby. His

freedom and the lifestyle he was used to before their one night of madness had gone for
ever. Yet he had concentrated all of his effort
into making this transition into married life
as easy as possible for her. She did not know
what was in it for him.

'Why are you doing all of this, Sam? We're
already married and we both know it's only
because of the baby.' Their food and drinks
arrived, and she had to wait until they were
alone again for his reply.

Sam took a forkful of his meal, prolonging
his answer. Emmy rested her head on both
hands, waiting. Eventually he stopped chew-
ing and swallowed.

'We rushed into this situation for the baby,
but it doesn't mean we should be miserable
for the rest of our lives. We've always enjoyed each other's company and it would be
a shame if that was no longer the case. I don't
want you to feel trapped or sad about the way
things have played out. If we're set on making
a safe and secure environment for our child,
that starts with us. We owe it to ourselves to
make this work and I'll take whatever steps
necessary for you to forgive me. We wouldn't

be in this situation if it wasn't for my selfishness and I'm sorry I ruined everything.'

Emmy could not even think of eating when she was trying to digest everything Sam said. Yes, she was unhappy, but it was not because of anything he had done. Rather, because of what he could not do. Love her. That was not his fault.

'I think we both played a part in what happened and how we're dealing with it. There's no need to play the martyr, Sam. We're in this together.' They both had to accept where they were now. She reached her hand across the table and he sandwiched it between both of his.

Emmy looked up and caught Sam's gaze. A current passed between them, something she thought she recognised from their last infamous night together. A hunger, a need for something more satisfying than a simple stew. That zap of electricity shot through her whole being, starting where her fingers were entwined with his. Sam was not backing away from the crazy sexual energy zinging between them either.

Emmy's heart was hammering at the impli-

cation he might want more than a platonic relationship after all and wondered if that would
heal or fracture her poor heart even more.

CHAPTER EIGHT

SAM LONGED TO kiss his wife. No one would blink an eye if he leaned across the table and captured her mouth with his. Especially when Emmy was looking at him like that was exactly what she wanted too. Except he was not going to repeat the mistake of rushing things without thinking them through first.

It seemed absurd that a little thing such as kissing Emmy should cause such overthinking when they were already married and expecting a family, but this was not any ordinary relationship. There was too much history on the line if he got things wrong again. They could not afford an ill-judged fling they could not walk away from when, back in the real world, Emmy would remember why she'd never wanted a relationship with him. In the city of romance it was understandable they might get caught up in the fantasy, but he was not going to be the one to encourage or initiate another flirtation with disaster.

'Emmy, I—' Sam sat back, getting ready to explain why this was not a good idea, and saw the shame washing over her features. Given the choice she would not want a relationship with him. The only reason she was leaning towards it now was because she was trapped with him. Perhaps in time he could show her he had left his old ways behind and she might learn to love him. For now though, this was mere fantasy they could not simply wish into existence.

As they sat staring at their still-full plates, a piercing scream cut through the pained silence. He looked up to see the other diners rushing from their tables, chairs overturning in their haste to get somewhere else.

'What's going on?' Emmy's hands went to her belly, her concern and instinct for her child blazing brightly in the face of any trouble.

Sam got to his feet to check what was causing the commotion, ready to get Emmy to safety if necessary.

He could see that blasted scooter, which had nearly clipped Emmy earlier, lying halfway across the road, the traffic stalled in both directions as a result. 'It looks like there's been a road accident. I'll go and see if anyone's been injured or if I can help.'

'I'll come with you.' Emmy pushed her chair out from the table and followed him through the maze of tables and people now spilling out onto the road.

Sam did not waste time on a futile attempt to talk her out of it when it was ingrained into both of them to provide medical assistance where it was needed. There were a lot of raised French voices mixed in with faint cries and groaning coming from the concentrated circle of people standing around.

'*Excusez-moi. Je suis un medecin.*' He eased his way through the crowd, reaching a hand back for Emmy to grab so he could lead her safely to the scene.

The long-haired teenager who had been riding the scooter was sitting on the ground, apparently in shock, with his head in his hands. Sam heard Emmy gasp when he saw why. A little girl, no more than five or six, was lying splayed on the road near the scooter with whom he assumed was the mother weeping at her child's side.

'Que s'est-il passé?' He asked the father, who was shouting for help, what had happened.

Although Sam had a good grasp of the French language, he had to ask the man to slow down so he could better understand him. After confirming he had phoned for an ambulance, he was able to tell Sam that the guy had been riding the scooter on the pavement. Going at some considerable speed he had lost control, and had clipped the little girl, knocking her into oncoming traffic.

Sam knelt down on the tarmac to take her pulse. A difficult task when she was wedged under the bumper of the car which had hit her.

'Comment t'appelles-tu?'

When there was no response from the girl, her father said, *'Elle s'appelle Amelie.'*

'Amelie? Je m'appelle Sam.'

He was not sure if she could hear him but he did not want to frighten her as he tried to scoot under the vehicle on his back, to reach her and carry out a primary survey of her condition. Her head was millimetres away from the front wheel and luckily the driver had stopped abruptly, narrowly avoiding crushing her skull.

As she was unresponsive, he moved quickly to check her airways were clear and tilt her head back. It was an uneasy scramble to get close enough to hear if she was breathing but somehow he managed it. Listening intently and watching the slight rise and fall of her chest, Sam established she was thankfully still breathing.

His next check was to look for signs of bleeding and it was then he noticed her blond hair stained crimson. If she had a head injury of some sort they could not move her without running the risk of causing further damage. They would have to wait until the paramedics arrived to stabilise her neck and spine before attempting to get her out. The fire brigade might have to be involved too, depending on how difficult that would prove to be. All he could do in the meantime was try to prevent her from going into shock from loss of blood and make sure she was breathing.

Sam lifted her legs and set them on top of his, elevating them above the level of her heart to keep the blood circulating and prevent organ failure. He tore off one sleeve of his shirt and used it to apply pressure to her head wound and stem the bleeding as best he could.

The gravel on the road was scratching at his back, the underbelly of the car so close to his face it was making him claustrophobic, but his discomfort came second to saving a child's life.

'Emmy, are you there?' He could not lift his head to see anything and was relying on her being nearby to hear him.

'Yes.' The flash of bright pink in his peripheral vision made him believe she was crouching down beside him, awaiting instruction.

'She's unconscious but she's got a pulse. Can you pass that on to the parents?' While he made sure the child's clothing was loose around her neck and there was nothing blocking her airways, he could hear a muffled, stilted conversation as Emmy tried to relay the information to the couple.

'Sam? I've got a blanket to put over her to keep her warm.' Emmy stretched under the car and covered the little girl with a tartan picnic rug she must have commandeered from someone to do the job.

'That's great.' It was also important to keep

the child's body temperature up in case she went into shock. He was glad to have Emmy's reassuring presence so close to him too, reminding him he was not alone in the dark with this girl's life in his hands.

'The boy on the scooter was wearing a helmet so he's relatively unscathed save for his skinned knees and hands. A little shaken but he's not badly hurt.' Emmy had clearly gone to the rider's assistance as he tended to Amelie. Whilst Sam was glad they were not dealing with two seriously injured adolescents, he was angered by the reckless behaviour which had caused the accident. It could have been Emmy if he had not pulled her to safety. The thought of her and the baby lying under the wheels of a car was enough to make a grown man weep and he was thankful he was not going through what Amelie's parents were right now.

'Let's hope it makes him think twice about racing around the streets in future. I'm going to stay here with Amelie until the emergency services get here to make sure there is no change to her breathing.' This was someone's baby, and though he was not yet a father, he would be devastated if anything should happen to his child. It made him wonder why his father had such a lack of interest in his own offspring. He had been able to float between families, somehow managing to neglect both. Hopefully the fact that Sam already cared about the welfare of his unborn child meant that he had not inherited all of his father's caddish, selfish ways after all.

He brushed the bloody strands of hair away from Amelie's face, imagining if this was Emmy or their baby lying here hovering between life or death. 'I'm here for you, sweetheart. I'm not going anywhere until I know you are safe.'

He reached out, took her tiny hand in his and squeezed. The closest he could get to giving her some comfort in the dark. When he felt the faintest twitch of her fingers against his palm it was like winning the lottery. Whatever the future held for him and Emmy as parents, he knew it was going to be one hell of an emotional carnival ride. He just hoped he remained strapped in until the music stopped playing.

It was getting dark by the time the drama had ended. Emmy let Sam do the talking with the

French paramedics as they carefully lifted little Amelie into the ambulance. The bistro insisted on waiving their payment for all the medical assistance they had provided but neither of them had any appetite after what they had seen.

They had walked away from the scene to get a little breathing space, but Emmy stopped to look at him closer under one of the streetlights.

'You are covered in oil and dirt.' The evidence of the trouble he had gone to in aiding the little girl was there in his torn shirt and the scrapes on his face too.

Sam shrugged. 'It's not important. All that matters is that she pulls through.'

'Of course, but you look like you were in a car accident too. Let me get you cleaned up a bit.' She led him over to the beautifully lit fountain in the square they'd wandered into and forced him to sit on the wall surrounding the pool of water.

He had been subdued since the paramedics had taken Amelie to the hospital, and she was worried about him. Although it was natural to be upset over an injured child, they dealt with that sort of incident every day during the course of their work. She wondered what made this one different.

'She was so still…' Sam was staring off somewhere into the distance and Emmy had to consider the possibility he was experiencing some sort of emotional shock.

'But she was breathing, and you did everything you could to comfort her.' She had seen the way he had held her hand and heard him whisper encouraging words to the child. It was a softer side to Sam she had never seen before. Yes, he had always treated her with kindness, but she had never been able to picture him getting soppy over children. For someone who had never wanted to be burdened with a family, he clearly had some paternal instincts, different from those in his paediatrician role. There was an emotional attachment there which was affecting him deeply. It had not been a pleasant scene, but it did give Emmy some confirmation that he had it in him to be a caring father, despite his own experiences growing up.

'Let's hope it was enough. All I could think about was that it could have been you, or our child, lying there. I don't know what I would do if I lost either of you.'

'Same.' Emmy exchanged a lopsided smile with him, overwhelmed by both his sudden outpouring of emotion and her own, having to imagine the worst happening.

She took a handkerchief from her handbag and dipped it into the rippling water behind them. After tilting Sam's face towards her, she began cleaning the evidence of his heroism away as best she could.

'I'm more invested in this little family of ours than I thought,' he said, his eyes locked onto hers, watching her intently.

Emmy's heart did a backflip, but she tried not to get her hopes up too much in case it was simply the emotional aftershock of the accident talking.

'I know it's probably too late to ask this but why have you been so against a family up until now?' When he had no choice but to get on board with the idea.

He dropped his gaze then. 'You know about my dad and his other family, how much it affected me and my mum. It wasn't only the cheating and lying, he treated all the people he was supposed to love with apathy. He gave no thought to our feelings or how we were surviving when he wasn't there. I never wanted to do that, to inflict so much pain on my own flesh and blood, no matter how unintentional.'

Emmy had no idea his thoughts on the subject ran so deep. She had always assumed his preference for a single life was based solely on having the freedom to behave as badly or wildly as he wished. Not that he was trying to avoid hurting people simply by living life. It was both endearing and tragic that he had been willing to sacrifice so much.

'You know that belief alone means you're nothing like him. That was a selfless decision you made, unnecessarily in my opinion, because you were considerate of other people's feelings. From everything I've heard about your father, and know about you, Sam, you're the antithesis of him.' This insight into Sam's psyche explained so much about his personal life and why he had never entered into a serious relationship. If he had not been so traumatised by his childhood, he might have settled down with someone else by now. It was only that legacy of guilt and fear left to him by his father which had led him here, with her.

'I'd like to think so but there are no guarantees.'

'You mean I don't get an exchange or a refund if you're defective?' Emmy employed some humour to deflect from her own burden of guilt that she had in some way benefitted from Sam's hang-ups.

''Fraid not. Sold as seen. So, there you go, that's a peek inside my messed-up world. Too late as it turns out, now we're already married.'

'We all have our issues. Why else would two otherwise sane individuals enter into a marriage without even going on a proper date?' Emmy knew to anyone else this set-up was beyond bizarre, and if her family had a hint about what was going on, they would have talked them out of this crazy scheme. Perhaps that was why she had not let them in on the wedding plans beforehand. In case they tried to reason with her, when logic had little to do with her choosing to marry Sam.

'At least we know we're both insane. Aren't you angry about what happened? This was my idea, but you didn't have to go along with it. Surely you dreamed about being madly in love with the man you married. You could have waited for him to come and sweep you off your feet.'

Emmy could not tell him he was the man of her dreams and spoil his version of events where they were both tragic characters miscast in this relationship. It would alter this fragile one they already had if he thought she might have orchestrated this whole thing to get him to marry her.

'With my dating history, a dream is all it ever could have been. As far as my exes were concerned, I wasn't marriage material. Just good for a laugh and a casual fling.'

'Then you were clearly dating the wrong men if they didn't value you for who you are.'

'Yeah, well, I'm used to it. I'm the family joke, as well you know.' Her hackles were up now, as she was reminded of all the times she'd been the butt of people's jokes or used and tossed aside when she was no longer deemed useful. It was no wonder she had decided that a marriage based on convenience was better than getting into another doomed love affair. At least what she had with Sam was honest, apart from her hiding the fact she had been madly in love with him for years.

'Why do you put up with that? You are far

from the doormat you let your sisters walk all over, and if that's how you let men treat you, it's no surprise you haven't found anyone suitable. You're not that subservient person who kowtows to everyone else's whim.'

'Aren't I?' When it came to relationships with family and boyfriends, that was exactly who she became. Afraid if she did not act the way they wanted her to, that they would cast her aside the way her birth parents had done.

'Not with me.'

It was only when Sam said it, she realised the truth in those words. With him she had never been afraid that he would abandon her for simply being herself. Until now. Ironically, if she did open up about how she truly felt about him it would make him think twice about being with her. Especially after he had shared his own fears. He would be worried more than ever about hurting her if he was incapable of returning those feelings.

'Well, you're like part of the furniture. I don't have to worry about impressing you.'

'Nice,' he said, rolling his eyes at her.

'You know what I mean. It doesn't matter what I say or do, you've never been mean to me. There was no need to change who I was around you.' As she said it, the reason she had harboured a crush on him all this time was there, shining bright. Sam accepted her unconditionally.

'I never had reason to be mean to you and neither does anyone else. Why don't you see that?' He reached up and stopped her tending his wounds so she would focus on what he was saying.

It was too much for her to simply accept his word as the truth. There had to be something about her which made everyone in her life turn their backs on her at some point. Even with him, now, she was waiting for the inevitable rejection once he got bored of her too.

'Clearly there's something wrong with me. My own parents gave me away once they were sick of me. They raised me for three years. If there had been any sort of bond there it should have broken their hearts to do that. No, it seems to have been a relief since they never made any attempt to reconnect or get me back. As for the Jenningses, as good as they were to take me in, I wasn't enough for them, and they went on to have the twins. I'm sure if they'd known that would happen they would never have considered adopting someone else's discarded child. I must be really hard work or plain irritating.' All of the feelings she had been holding back for years came tumbling out of her mouth in the wake of Sam's honesty. She did not know if it was going to make him see her any differently other than to think she was more of a basket case than ever. By telling him all of this she was highlighting all the inadequacies which had caused people in her life to abandon her, providing Sam with reasons to do the same.

'Well, you are pretty annoying at times...' Sam was grinning at her and not taking her concerns about her personal defects seriously at all.

Emmy scooped some water from the fountain and flicked it at him. 'I'm pouring my heart out to you here. At least pretend you're interested.'

'Sorry, but you know this is completely neurotic, right? You were a child. All kids are a pain at times, but their parents don't simply sign them away. It's your parents who were the waste of skin, not you, and the Jenningses absolutely adore you. Your mum, dad and Dave would lay down their lives for you. The twins, probably not so much, but they're spoiled and immature. Again, their problem, not yours. Someday they'll grow up and see what an amazing sister they have in you.'

'If I'm such a great person, then why couldn't I find someone who wanted to marry me for real? It took a family friend getting me knocked up at a wedding reception to warrant even a half-baked proposal.'

Sam flinched at her caustic take on their situation but on the surface that was all it had been.

'You've sold yourself too short for too long, Emmy. I don't know who else didn't treat you the way you deserved but perhaps you were following the pattern your birth parents set. You got involved with men who thought you weren't worth a commitment but, in reality, it was the other way around. They never deserved you. Neither do I.' He took the hand which she had been tending to his injuries with and kissed it. It was all very romantic, everything she could have dreamed of, but that was the problem.

'You never would have married me if it wasn't for the baby.' That was what it came down to in the end for Emmy. They were only here because of a mistake and nothing else.

'Maybe not but I wouldn't have married anyone else, I can guarantee you that. You are the only woman I could ever have imagined spending the rest of my life with because we know each other so well. Okay, so we kept a few of our personal neuroses quiet until now, but I'm sure we can work our way around that along with everything else.'

Emmy was in danger of sliding off the wall and drowning in the fountain as Sam completely melted her defences. 'What are you saying?'

'That maybe we should give this marriage thing a try for real.' He dropped her hand, only to caress her cheek instead.

Emmy leaned into the palm of his hand, her eyes closed, as she let herself believe they had a chance together, when he was telling her the next best thing to 'I love you.'

CHAPTER NINE

SAM WAS SAILING close to the wind. If he got this wrong in any way, this relationship would be over before it properly began. Marriage had been pushing them apart and tonight, opening up, and listening to Emmy's fears in return, made him realise he could not lose her or what they had together. He had been trying to keep his feelings for her in check but tonight had been his undoing. The emotional fallout from the accident and realising how lost he would be without Emmy had made Sam face up to what was happening.

There was a chemistry between them they could no longer ignore, and the way Emmy was responding to him now, burrowing into his palm like a pussycat, said she felt the same way. By denying it he was afraid they were hurting each other more. They had not discussed physical intimacy within their marriage, but they were only human. Recent history had proven that in the bedroom they could set the sheets on fire. This time they did not have to worry about the consequences. Other than him falling any deeper for Emmy than he already had.

With her eyes still closed, pressed into him, she looked more content and happier than he had seen her in a while. Like a moth to a flame he was drawn to her smiling mouth, brushing his lips softly across hers. She accepted him quickly, kissing him back, and beginning that tugging sensation within him, begging for more.

With both hands now cradling her face and pulling her closer, he deepened the kiss. This was not the way either of them had pictured their lives turning out, but she was his and he was hers now. They did not have to hold back, and after everything she had told him about her past lovers, there was no reason to. Tonight, he would show her how perfect she was to him.

'Mrs Goodwin, would you like to take this back to the honeymoon suite?' His voice was ragged with the raw lust pumping in his veins for her. If she had any doubt about how much he wanted her she only had to listen.

Her eyes popped open, her pupils dark with the same need. She bit her bottom lip as she nodded her head, that urgency for intimacy overriding any bashfulness. That coy exterior did not last for long when Emmy was in the throes of passion and Sam was keen to get her there soon.

He stood up, bowed and held out his hand *à la* a Regency suitor expressing his interest in a twirl around the ballroom floor. Emmy giggled, kicked up her heels with a squeal and accepted his invitation with a curtsey. This was exactly why they were so good together. They were both incorrigible dorks.

The childish behaviour was soon replaced with that of a more mature nature. As they strolled back to the hotel, their path illuminated by the lights of the Eiffel Tower, they finally let the romantic mood consume them. Hand in hand, lips on lips, they stumbled towards the consummation of their marriage. Stopping every now and then, disappearing down a cobbled alleyway when Sam could not contain his need for her a second longer. The passionate interludes—mouths meshing, tongues clashing, hands searching under clothes for that skin-on-skin contact—made their journey twice as long. It also hiked up the expectation of what was to come in that honeymoon suite. Foreplay without either of them being naked.

'*Bonsoir,*' he said to the evening reception-ist when they finally reached the hotel, before they rushed up the flight of stairs to their room. His heart was racing, breathing rapid, as the blood pumped furiously to all parts of his body in anticipation.

The last time he and Emmy had shared a bed they had not had the luxury of time or spending a night together. Although their tryst then had been a frenzied feast of fun, tonight he was going to slow the pace so they could properly enjoy one another. After making love for the first time as husband and wife, he hoped it would prove enjoyable enough for Emmy to want to continue a real relationship with him for a long time to come.

Emmy was breathless with excitement as they fell into their room in between a flurry of kisses. This was not their first time together, but it had all the build-up of a new relationship when they had so much to prove to each other in bed. That their last foray into a hotel bedroom had not been a fluke in its explosive display of fiery passion. If they were going to entertain the idea of a physical arrangement in the marriage, it was necessary that they could maintain that level of chemistry and enjoy a healthy sex life. After a lifetime of lusting after Sam, she was sure she would not have a problem keeping her side of the bargain, but she could not say the same for him.

It was one thing having an exciting, illicit hook-up, during someone else's wedding reception, praying no one noticed their absence. Quite another sleeping with the same person for the rest of their lives. If tonight was a flop and did not meet expectations, it could jeopardise everything. It might make Sam think twice about this addendum to the contract. The pressure alone of making him think she was worth sacrificing all other women was making her doubt the validity of that.

'Hey. Stop thinking. I can see those cogs whirring.' Sam called her out, knowing her well enough to understand what was going on in her head.

'I just…' She could not find the words to

tell him she was afraid their next move could be the wrong one, even when it felt so right.

'Shh.' He put his finger on her lips. 'There's no need to overanalyse this or worry about what happens next. We're married. We shouldn't have to concern ourselves with the morning after the night before, only feel, enjoy, be together.'

It was a convincing argument. Especially when he was dotting kisses across her neck and her mind could only focus on the butterfly sensation of his lips flitting over her skin.

'What if—?' She attempted to ask what would happen if he could never learn to love her and the sex was just that, an act without emotion—could they survive on that alone? But he cut her off with a kiss, stealing the words from her lips with his, and reminding her to live in the moment. All her concerns about the future could wait until she could think straight again, when she was not distracted by Sam stroking her bare skin under her clothes, making her want to get naked right now.

'What if we simply enjoy our honeymoon and leave everything else until we get back home?' He lifted her top over her head and stripped off what was left of his shirt.

'Sounds good to me,' she said, breathlessly, with Sam busy undoing the buttons on her skirt, leaving her standing in nothing but her underwear. Thank goodness for the rush of blood to the head she had in the airport when she had splashed out on an expensive navy lace and silk set in place of her comfortable favourites. She had not predicted him seeing her in them but figured having something sexy close to her skin would make her feel better. How right she had been.

'You look amazing.' Sam confirmed she had made the right choice, kissing her shoulders as he slid the straps of her bra down her arms.

Emmy shivered, felt her nipples harden against their silky confines, then gasped when Sam bit gently on one puckered nub. She braced herself on his shoulders to remain upright as he peeled her underwear away so he could take her fully in his mouth. With her breast in his hand he licked and sucked her pink tip until she thought she would orgasm from that sensation of his rolling tongue and grazing teeth alone. There was an impatient second when he took time to release the clasp on her bra but only for a short time as he resumed his attention on her other breast. Her legs were quivering, her body aching with need for him, but she did not want this to end.

She let her hands do the talking, deftly unbuttoning his trousers and pushing them and his boxer shorts down his legs. Sam kicked them off so he was gloriously naked in front of her, as big and proud as she remembered. Eager to please him the same way he had done for her, Emmy kneeled before him. She saw that flare of desire in his eyes and smiled, knowing she put it there. With the flat of her tongue, she licked the full length of his shaft, the muscles of his thighs tensing under her hands as she did so.

She moved one hand to take hold of his erection, slipping up and down the smooth ridged skin to make him groan. Full of confidence and bravado, she stared up at him as she took him into her mouth. His eyes almost rolling back in his head as she swirled her tongue around his engorged member.

'Emmy—' His ragged warning only emboldened her, taking him deeper into her mouth, her throat, to enjoy him fully.

He thrust his hips with his next groan, and she tasted the salty evidence of his arousal. Sam's hands were tugging her hair, urging her up on to her feet again.

'Do you know what you're doing to me, Emmy?'

'Probably the same as you're doing to me.' She took his hand and slid it onto her panties so he could feel the wetness there for himself.

With a guttural groan he whipped them off and hoisted her leg up onto his hip. One breath-stealing thrust, and he was inside her, filling her, completing her. His sigh of satisfaction matched her own now they were finally joined together.

Emmy wound her arms around his neck and Sam hitched her other leg around his waist. He carried her over to the bed without breaking the connection between their bodies. The rose petals on the covers were cool against her skin, their perfume adding to the romance of the moment. It was easy to believe this was their honeymoon and forget the disaster of their actual wedding night. How she longed for everything they had in Paris to fly back home with them.

'I'm not hurting you, am I?' Sam asked as he lowered his body on top of hers.

'No.' That weight of him was wanted. She revelled in that feel of him pressing down on her, cocooning her. Being his.

He moved slowly at first, letting her get accustomed to having him fill her again after such a long time. Emmy closed her eyes and luxuriated in that most intimate of acts. The sensation of Sam's hot breath on her neck, his thighs brushing against hers, was almost enough for her to completely unravel. Then he was kissing her again, kneading her tender breast in his large palm and sending her into more raptures.

Emmy was a banquet stretched out before him. So many delicious tastes to savour. Every sample he took making him yearn for more. The kiss on her neck, the lick of a taut nipple, brought soft content moans to her lips. A sound which he wanted to hear again and again, knowing this was one area he could please her.

Sam slowly withdrew from her slick core and slid down the bed until his head was buried between her soft thighs. He filled her again, this time with his tongue. Using it to reach deep inside, swirling around that most sensitive spot, until she was calling out his name and arching off the bed.

Before she came back to earth, Sam thrust his hips and slid his straining erection into her wetness. That evidence of her orgasm strengthening his arousal, driving him faster towards his own satisfaction. Emmy too was urging his pace with her panting breaths at his ear and her nails raking over his back. She wanted him to reach that pinnacle with her and he was only too pleased to play catch-up. That pressure building inside him was allowed to break free, his climax taking everything in him and leaving him collapsed on top of Emmy, unable to move.

'That was…can't catch my breath…you're amazing.' His head was nestled against her breast so he could feel her chest rising and falling as she fought to get her breathing under control.

'So are you.' She kissed the top of his head, making him smile.

Given the choice right now he would happily make love to this one woman for the rest of his life. As someone who had let her down from the start he couldn't say for sure if he alone would ever be enough for her. All he could do was hope this feeling of euphoria they had created in each other would last.

At least for this weekend they were living as a couple, far from the everyday worries they would have to face back home with the reality of their arrangement. Combining work and raising a child together could test the strongest of relationships. Their now not-so-convenient marriage might not survive the strain when one of the party had feelings for the other.

It took a few moments for Emmy to realise where she was when she woke up, wondering if she was imagining the over-the-top boudoir. Then she remembered she was on honeymoon with Sam and rolled over with a lascivious grin on her face. It quickly disappeared when she found his side of the bed empty. She sat up, clutching the silk sheets to her naked body, looking to see if his things had gone too. The only clothes strewn recklessly across the floor were hers.

All at once, her fears came rushing in, shoving away her happy thoughts. Perhaps in the morning light he had regretted cross-ing that line with her and wanted to put some space between them. She did not think he would have gone home without her but even going for a walk without telling her was a warning sign that all was not well.

Last night she had been on top of the world, feeling loved in every way possible. She should have known it was too good to be true. Today she was right back down to earth, scrabbling to get back on her feet and face the world again. She hoped whatever problem had developed while she had been sleeping, Sam would have the decency not to share it. They were supposed to be putting on a united front and she would be humiliated if he had left a message at reception ultimately rejecting her.

She was deciding whether to get dressed and packed right away or take a shower first when the door opened. When Sam walked into the room carrying two takeaway cups in his hands and a paper bag in his mouth, she burst into noisy tears.

He dropped the bag on the bed and set the drinks on the bedside table. 'What? What's happened?'

She was trying to smile through the relieved sobbing and was sure she looked grotesque in the process. 'I thought you'd gone.'

He frowned at her as he came to sit on the bed. 'Why on earth would I do that?'

'I thought you regretted last night.' She was afraid to look at him in case there was any element of truth in her fear.

'Er, why would I do that when I had the time of my life? You really need to start trusting I'm not going to run out on you. I'm not your parents or one of your ex-boyfriends. I'm your husband.' He caught her chin between his finger and thumb and forced her to look at him, to believe in what he was telling her.

As well as his sincerity, she swore she could see disappointment in those big eyes that she should think so badly of him after everything he had done to make her comfortable in this relationship.

'I'm sorry. It's just going to take some time for me to get used to that.' To trusting someone.

'You were sleeping. I only left the bed to get breakfast from that bakery we saw yesterday. I thought you deserved the real deal this morning. Freshly made croissants from the *boulangerie*. I would never go anywhere without you. Especially when you're here lying naked in bed.' He tugged his shirt over his head and scrambled in beside her. Emmy let out a squeal of delight as he caught hold of her for a kiss. He tasted of minty tooth-paste and promises, and she relaxed into his embrace once more.

'What about breakfast?' she asked with a pout.

'Sod breakfast. There's only one thing I'm hungry for this morning and that's you.' Sam pretended to nibble on her neck, making her laugh and forget all her insecurities in the process.

'I could get used to this,' Emmy sighed, leaning back against Sam's solid chest. He squeezed the sponge over her shoulders and let the soapy hot water cascade over her breasts.

'Don't get too used to it. Our flight is first thing in the morning.' He kissed the side of her neck and wrapped his arms around her.

'Nah-nah-nah. I'm not listening.' She stuck her fingers in her ears so she would not hear things she did not want to.

'Idiot,' he said, somewhere outside of the white noise in her head.

She turned and stuck out her tongue at him, only for Sam to grab her legs and twist the rest of her body around so she was effectively straddling him.

'That's better.' His voice had already changed from teasing her to wanting her.

'Again?' She could barely believe it when they had spent most of the day already making love. Not that she was complaining. She had been content lying here in the bath with him, looking out at the spectacular view and listening to the busy world outside. To some it might have seemed like a wasted opportunity not leaving the hotel room to visit the city she had longed to see for so long but spending this time with Sam had been so much more important to her. She might never have this again with him. Despite everything he had said, neither of them could promise this marriage would last for ever.

'It's our honeymoon. If you are able to walk by the end of it, we're doing something wrong.' Sam's casual tease took her breath away again before he carried her back to bed. They did not bother to dry off first.

This time making love was a long, leisurely affair. Lying on their sides, looking into one another's eyes, Sam took her body with his once more. Each time felt like the first, every thrust of him inside her a surprise and delight. With her limbs wrapped around his body, Emmy knew she was exactly where she wanted to be.

CHAPTER TEN

'STOP KICKING THE man's chair, Stevie.'

'No.'

'Do as you're told, or I'll confiscate your games console.'

'You're too hard on him, Dan.'

'Well, one of us has to discipline him and you let him get away with murder.'

Sam listened to the family argue in the row behind them, his head banging off his chair with every thump of their child's foot against his seat. He did his best to grit his teeth and ignore it but the family dynamic going on was making him more uncomfortable in more ways than one.

Emmy was sleeping against the plane window, with little wonder. They had worn each other out in bed over the weekend. Although he wished they'd had longer to get to know each other before returning to normal life.

Despite being in each other's lives for so long, there was still a lot about each other they apparently did not know. He would never have known Emmy was dealing with such deep-rooted issues around feelings of abandonment if she had not shared that information over the course of the trip.

That was obviously something that still affected her in her adult life, just as his hang-ups about his father continued to dominate his life decisions. If he had been aware that it was an ongoing problem with Emmy, he might have thought twice about the wedding. He ran the risk of hurting her even more if he could not give her everything she needed from him. Now he was worried more than ever about repeating his father's mistakes.

He had every intention of taking care of his family and being there for Emmy and his child, but as he had found, life did not always go to plan. What if work took up more time than he could devote to school plays or sports days? What if he and Emmy discovered down the line that a physical relationship was not enough to sustain their marriage? The fallout from any breakdown in their relationship was going to affect them and their child, however hard they tried to avoid it. Sam wondered if he was courting even more trouble by sparking a sexual relationship with Emmy. Once they were home she would expect them to move into one bedroom, intensifying their bond, and putting more pressure on him to be the perfect husband. There was a reason he had never wanted to get married and this was it. Too much expectation for him to possibly ever live up to, and after the euphoria of this mini-break, it felt as though he could only go down in Emmy's estimation from now.

'I need the toilet.'

'Dan, you take him.'

'I always have to take him.'

'I'm so sorry it's too much to ask for you to take your son to the toilet. I'll do it, shall I? Like everything else.'

'I work, Sharon.'

'And I don't? At least you get paid and have time away from the house…'

The family who had probably spent an enjoyable break at a theme park or the beach began to descend into a domestic row as they faced their imminent return home.

Suddenly the plane felt very claustrophobic with Sam trapped, listening to his worst fears play out in real time.

'I'll see you later, then,' Emmy called as she got out of the car. There was no fond farewell or goodbye kiss from her husband before he drove on to find a parking space. She was left standing there in the dust watching him leave, trying to figure out what she had done wrong.

It had been this way since their return from honeymoon. That period of their marriage apparently well and truly over. She had tried to ask him about it and why things had changed so dramatically between them but the only answer he could give her was that he was busy and tired. Except the distance had been there since the moment they had stepped off the plane, back on home soil.

Her idea, or the one he had led her to believe was true, that they would continue their loved-up relationship from where they had left off in that Parisian hotel room, could not have been further from the truth. There were no more shared baths or nights cuddled up together in bed. If anything, Sam seemed to be avoiding her. His shifts usually conflicting with hers, and on evenings where they were alone together, he always had paperwork to catch up on in another room away from her.

She went to bed at night wanting to cry herself to sleep but found herself too empty inside to summon the tears. This was her life from now on and though she had seen it coming, she had tried to pretend they were making it work. She did not even have friends or family to confide in with the truth. Her colleagues believed her life with Sam was something out of a romance novel, and if the truth came out to her parents or David, they would be devastated by the betrayal. They were invested in the relationship between her and one of their trusted friends. If it came down to it she could not be sure they would take her side in the break-up. She could imagine the conversations would remind her Sam was a dishy doctor, a catch way too good for the likes of her, and she should consider herself lucky he had 'taken her on.' In their eyes she would be the one in the wrong. She always had been when it came down to taking sides between her and anyone close.

Rows over stolen make-up or clothes ruined with the twins when they were growing up had all been ruled in Lorna's and Lisa's favour when their parents got involved.

'You should be pleased they want to be like you...'

'They don't know any better...'

'I'm sure they didn't mean to do it...'

An argument with Sam would no doubt have the same result with her being the one urged to work harder to make things right, to make life easier for everyone else. Her feelings never seemed to be taken into consideration against anyone else's. As though she was acceptable collateral damage in the scheme of things. Easier to hurt her than real family.

Sometimes she thought they considered Sam more a part of that than she was when they went out of their way to make him feel comfortable. Usually she simply put up and shut up. Yet as her pregnancy progressed and her marriage stalled, Emmy knew she could not continue this way for much longer. Living like this was making her more miserable than if she had been left alone to raise the baby. At least then she would not have been under any illusion that something was there between her and Sam.

In hindsight, it seemed the honeymoon had been to appease her after her post-wedding blues. It certainly had not been to develop any emotional ties when they were more distant than ever. She simply had to face the fact Sam had physical needs and she had satisfied them for a short while. It was difficult not to think about who might have taken her place since.

During their romantic getaway he had told her she was the only one he could have imagined marrying but not that she was the only woman he would sleep with. They did not have anything written on paper, nor had they discussed being monogamous, but she had hoped that would be part of the deal. Sam knew she did not sleep around but that was where they differed. She had become one of those women who had thought she could change her man with marriage and ended up disappointed to find out otherwise.

There was no proof he had embarked on an extramarital affair, but she had intimate knowledge of his rampant sexual appetite. Given they had not slept together since their return from Paris it was only a matter of time before he sought relief from another quarter. Sam would have the pick of more attractive, slimmer women than his pregnant wife, so he would have no reason to go without affection or intimacy. It was Emmy who would suffer, wondering every night he worked late who he was with and why it was not her.

When she started her shift, it was with a feeling of dread, knowing their marriage was over before it really began. Unless she could persuade her husband she was the only woman he needed in his life, her future was looking bleaker than ever. She did not want to bring a baby into their home with them living separate lives, its mother miserable and pining after someone who could not give her what she wanted. Sam had tried to warn her, explained why marriage was not for him, but she had gone willingly into his bed and there was no one but herself to blame for falling even deeper in love with him.

Tonight, she was going to tackle some big decisions. If she was going to make changes in her life, she had to do it now lest she left it too late. Prior to the baby's arrival and before there was nothing left of her shattered heart to piece together. She would seduce him, beg him to talk to her, do whatever it took to find out where they stood as a couple once and for all. If she didn't hear what she wanted, their marriage could be over before they hit their one-month anniversary. Confirmation she remained unloved and unwanted, that everyone left her in the end, and foolish to believe that Sam could see past her physical imperfections to a woman he could see a future with.

It would, however, make the twins' year.

This was killing him. Emmy had left a brief voice message on his phone asking him to make time for her tonight if possible. That said everything about the state of their so-called marriage. Yes, he had been avoiding her, for her own good. Now it seemed as though everything was about to come to a head, and he was going to lose her for ever. He could not expect her to carry on as they were when she was so unhappy, but there did not seem to be any other way to avoid hurting her except by keeping his distance. It was not fair to lead her on and pretend this was a proper marriage, or one in name only. They had fallen somewhere in between with messy emotions getting in the way of the hot sex and confusing everything. If they were splitting up it needed to be her decision, so she felt in control and not a victim. He did not want to be someone else to let her down and make her believe it was her fault. By bedding her he had simply hastened the end, knowing they were in deeper than they had intended but still pretending this was a marriage of convenience.

'Are you coming for drinks?' Ben, one of the nurses on the ward, asked as he gathered his stuff to go home.

'No. Emmy has something planned.'

Ben whistled.

'Lucky you. Make the most of it. As soon as the babies start coming you won't get the chance to plan any sexy time together.' He waggled his eyebrows suggestively, making Sam laugh at a time when it was the last thing he felt like doing.

'I will,' he said, already trying to find excuses to avoid *the talk*. They had not told anyone about the baby, so he knew Ben was only kidding around. Even if his words were hitting close to home.

Once sleep was scarce and tempers frayed, Emmy would resent being trapped in this marriage. He was worried he would too. Perhaps that was why his father had moved from house to house, family to family, never settling long enough to contribute anything valuable to any of them. If they could not admit this had been a mistake, they risked dragging this discontent through their child's life too, making them all unhappy in the long run.

'Dr Goodwin! I'm glad you're still here. Can you give us a hand with a young patient in A & E?' A visibly stressed nurse from paediatric A & E rushed into the staff room looking relieved she had got to him before he had left for the night.

Sam thought of Emmy waiting for him at home, anticipating his arrival and expecting an explanation for his recent behaviour. He wasn't a coward, but he knew what would always take priority and it was time they both realised it.

'Sure.' He did not even ask about the patient's condition first, sure it was where he had to be. They needed him, Emmy did not. He was never going to make the difference in her life he could make to his patients. Tonight, she would see that for herself.

'I waited up.'

'You didn't have to.' Sam took off his coat and slumped into the nearest armchair.

Emmy was sitting in the dark by the window, presumably watching for his car to pull up into the driveway. He had thought, hoped, she would have gone to bed by now, the case keeping him at the hospital until well past midnight.

'I was worried about you.' She had not even changed into her comfy pyjamas. Sam looked around to see if there were packed bags anywhere but saw nothing to indicate she had finally had enough of him.

'I told you I got caught up at work.' He was tired and irritable after a difficult night in the emergency room. It was the worst possible time to be having this conversation. Yes, he thought she would be better off without him but he did not want her to hate him. At the end of the day he was still the baby's father and it was important they could at least remain amicable. Things like sharing childcare or putting on a united front for special events in their baby's life would be difficult if she could not bear the sight of him.

'Yes, but I haven't heard anything from you since.' There was a steeliness to her voice in the shadows.

Although she could not see him, he shrugged

like it was no big deal. Making it clear he was not going to account for his whereabouts every minute of the day. Even wearing his father's attitude made his stomach roll but he reminded himself he was doing this for the better good. 'In case you've forgotten, we're not *really* married.'

'Oh.' Her simple exclamation sounded as though he'd punched her in the gut.

He had to steady himself on the arms of his chair so he would not rush to her and apologise on bended knee. Instead, he swallowed the bile in his throat and doubled down on the onslaught of blows. 'You had your little romantic trip but we're back in the real world now. I have other responsibilities and priorities. I thought you understood that, Emmy.'

'I thought… I thought after Paris we were going to make a go of this relationship and try to be a real couple.'

'Emmy, Emmy, Emmy. That was never on the cards. The very nature of our marriage is its convenience. That to me means continuing to live our separate lives whilst raising our child together.'

'For you that means sleeping with other people?'

He wanted to yell, 'No!' Instead, he said quietly, 'You knew who I was when you married me.'

The fact was she knew better now who he was but that was why he was doing this. She needed that nudge to realise sympathy was not a reason to excuse anything he did to cause her pain.

There was a pause. He thought he heard her sniffing and imagined her trying not to cry. Everything he had hoped to avoid with this stupid marriage contract in the first place. 'Then I'm afraid I can't do this, Sam. I can't stay married to you when it is making me so unhappy. It's not fair on anyone.'

The chair creaked as she stood but he did not get up. Neither did he attempt to convince her to stay. As her shadow crossed the room and out the door all he could say was, 'I'm sorry things turned out this way.'

The only true statement he had made since coming home.

Emmy could not bring herself to tell anyone about the break-up. Not anyone at work and certainly not family. There would be too many questions, and how could she explain what had happened without admitting that the whole marriage had been a sham? The only thing worse than everyone knowing her relationship with Sam had been fake was the realisation that she could not even make that work. There was surely nothing more pathetic than a woman who had married for security and it not lasting the month.

As a result of being unwilling to share her woes with anyone close, she had nowhere to go after walking out on Sam. It had been a necessary step, pre-empting the toxic atmosphere which would surely develop when things were already so fractured between them. She was at a loss to explain what had happened to them between the passionate kisses in Paris and the cold shoulder back home. Why he had changed so suddenly from a loving husband to someone she simply shared a house with. A virtual stranger to her but the person he had always told her he was when it came to women. She should never have convinced herself he was anything but that womaniser with no intention of settling down. At least she could protect their child from growing up in that environment which would inevitably have an impact, even if it was too late for her.

'Thank you for coming out at such short notice, Mr Sutherland. I really appreciate it.' After a few nights spent in a cheap hotel room, Emmy knew she had to find somewhere to live before her money ran out. She did not want to end up homeless and penniless before the baby arrived. Her parents' place would have been her absolute last resort. Thankfully, she had the brainwave of contacting her old landlord, who had yet to rent out her old flat to anyone else. Goodness knew what he thought about her returning so quickly and with a wedding ring on her finger, but he said nothing. Mr Sutherland did not say much as a rule.

'I ain't carrying anything for you. Here's the key. Rent's due at the end of the month,' he grunted, before shuffling off down the street.

'It's okay, I don't have much with me,' Emmy called after him. Despite his gruffness she was tempted to run after him and give him a hug. Getting her old place back was the one bright spot in the dark days which had followed her so-called honeymoon.

She twirled her Eiffel Tower key ring around her finger. Mr Sutherland had not bothered to take it off the flat key and she was happy to be reunited with it. A gift to herself long before babies and marriage had been on her radar. However, now she would associate it with bittersweet memories of seeing it for real.

She yawned. It was getting late and she was standing on the pavement with all of her worldly possessions packed into bags when all she wanted to do was climb into bed. With her rucksack and handbag over her shoulders, she extended the handle on her trolley bag and began dragging it up the steps. It was packed so full she had to walk backwards, hauling it with both hands. Next time she walked out on a marriage she would make sure to book a removal van first.

Once she was inside, she dropped everything on the floor, her muscles aching, and her lungs fit to burst as she flopped onto the couch. Her phone vibrated in her pocket, on silent so she would not have to deal with anyone. The endless vibration forced her to look at it. It was Sam calling.

'Ugh.' Emmy let her phone fall onto her

chest. There was no way she was answering that one after the way he had behaved. It was not as if he was going to apologise or beg for forgiveness. More than likely he was calling to have their marriage annulled, beg her not to tell David or to assert his rights over custody of their unborn baby. Given his sudden change from adoring spouse to wannabe bachelor, she remained sceptical that the responsible father act would last. For days she had wept over him, and did not owe him a conversation now.

The fact that he was working at the same hospital was going to make things awkward and difficult to avoid him for too long. With the personal leave she had taken now over, there were decisions to make, and actions to take before her pregnancy was too advanced to do anything. If he was not going anywhere, she might have to. Everything would come out eventually so she might have to bite the bullet and tell her family.

Perhaps it was time for a completely new start, transferring to another hospital while she juggled working with motherhood. As much as she wanted her mother and father to be hands-on grandparents, only too willing to babysit when needed, she could not rely on it.

How could she expect them to support her and love her baby when she had grown up doubting they felt that way about her? She was not going to subject her child to that sense of being the outsider in the family. If it came to it, Emmy would go it alone with her baby. After all, she was the only person she could truly rely on.

The phone buzzed again with a notification. Curiosity got the better of her when she saw her soon-to-be ex-husband had left her a voice message.

'It's Sam. I was hoping we could talk… I want to make sure you are all right. No one seems to know where you are and, well, I'm still the father of this baby. You know where I am.'

That was the crux of it all and she could not change the past, or biology, as much as she wished she could. Sam was the father, she was the mother, and whatever their relationship, she still wanted the best for her child. Whether that meant staying where she was and giving Sam a second chance to prove his worth, or moving away to start over on her own, remained to be seen.

Exhausted from her step backwards into singledom, she was too tired to make any more life changes tonight. She had waited a lifetime for Sam, now it was his turn to do the hanging around. As she drifted off to sleep, still on the sofa wearing her coat and shoes, a smile crossed her lips. Something she had feared she might never do again since leaving her husband.

CHAPTER ELEVEN

IT WOULD NOT be overdramatic for Sam to say he had become a shell of a man recently. Since driving Emmy away his conscience refused to let him sleep or eat properly. As a professional, he had managed to keep his private life separate from work and continued doing his job to the best of his abilities. That did not mean he was not worried sick about Emmy and the baby or that he did not regret how stupid he had been.

'Emmy, please talk to me…' He made another desperate plea to the voicemail on her phone. It had come as no surprise that she would not want contact with him after everything. In order to protect her from an unhappy life spent with him, he had pushed her away, but the scheme had proved too successful. She seemed to have vanished into thin air.

If he had not been so wrapped up in his

own loss, he might have realised there was something serious going on beyond his empty house and broken heart. It had taken him a few days of licking his wounds and feeling sorry for himself before trying to reach out to her. The continued silence had frightened him enough to swallow his pride and ask others if they had news of his wife's whereabouts.

'You've lost her already?' Shelley, one of the paediatric nurses who worked with Emmy, had quipped when he had begun searching for her in earnest.

'Yeah. Uh, we're taking some time out but I wanted to make sure she's okay.'

It came as a surprise to her colleagues to find out they had separated already, and Emmy would not be happy he had shared such personal information, but he was getting desperate by that stage. As it was, they could only tell him she had taken some personal leave.

The next logical place to try and locate her was at her parents' house. Whether she was there or not, he was not looking forward to the confrontation which would inevitably occur with his arrival. He was either already persona non grata, if the family had heard

Emmy's side of the story, or he was going to have to break it himself and land himself in the messy stuff.

This house had been a refuge to them both during their tumultuous childhoods. Today he was as anxious as though he was about to face a firing squad on the other side of that door. One deep breath in and he pushed the doorbell, reminding himself this was about his missing wife and unborn child. Not his popularity.

'Sam? What are you doing here? Is Emmy in the car?' It was Dave who opened the door, peering over his shoulder looking for his sister. That answered some questions. No, she was not here, and she had not told them about the break-up or the reasons behind it. It filled Sam with dread and his blood ran cold to discover Emmy really was missing.

'No. I'm afraid not. Can I come in?'

'Sure.' Dave stood aside to let him in, the frown burrowed into his forehead a sign he knew already there was something serious going on. Sam was not looking forward to confessing his darkest deeds to his oldest friend, but if that was what it took to keep Emmy safe, he would take the consequences on the chin. Literally, if he knew Dave as well as he thought he did.

'I wasn't expecting you to be here, mate, but I'm glad you are.' He needed some moral support as he faced his in-laws with the news that he had been so unkind to their daughter she had either run away or got into trouble. Either way, Sam was to blame. Although Dave would be mad at him, he was sure he would put that aside to concentrate on finding his little sister.

'I just called in to see the folks. What's up?' Dave led him into the living room, where Mr and Mrs Jennings were sitting enjoying a cup of tea.

'Hi, Sam. What brings you here?'

'Sit down. Is Emmy with you?'

Sam took a seat, sagging under the weight of guilt of ruining yet more lives. 'Um, I don't know how to put this to you, but Emmy's missing.'

'What do you mean she's missing?' Dave flopped down beside him on the sofa, making Sam aware of his bulk and concern at the same time.

Sam cleared his throat. 'She, uh, we, uh, agreed to part.'

He was tempted to close his eyes to shut out the pain and confusion he could see on all three faces peering at him.

Eventually it was Mrs Jennings who threw her hands up and laughed. 'All couples fight. You'll kiss and make up soon enough. How many times have we argued and threatened to walk out?'

No one in the room returned her too bright smile.

'I get the feeling this isn't the same thing Sam's talking about.' Mr Jennings looked a lot sterner about the news.

'You've only been married five minutes. What did you do?' Dave's hard stare would have been intimidating enough without the clenched fists and Sam was already bracing himself for the inevitable hit.

'Things would never have worked out between us. We just figured that out too late. Anyway, that's not the point. I haven't heard from her since and it's been days. I'm worried something might have happened to her. Especially if she hasn't been in touch with you guys.' The family had been his last stop. With them in the dark as much as he was, he might have to make things official and report her disappearance to the police.

'Woah. Hold up. You can't simply drop that on us and expect us not to have questions. Emmy idolises you, bro, she always has, so I'm assuming you did something to upset her?'

Sam was too busy processing Dave's revelation to defend himself.

'Emmy *idolises* me? Since when?' It was news to him, but he was not simply going to take her brother's word on that score when he was completely unaware of the true nature of their relationship.

'Are you serious? You're married, for goodness' sake. If you don't know she's been in love with you since she was a kid, then it's no wonder things aren't working out. You're an idiot.' With that, Dave got up and crossed the room away from him, his phone to his ear. Presumably trying to get hold of Emmy himself.

Sam looked to her parents for confirmation that this was not simply some wild theory Dave had conjured up to make him feel even worse than he already did. They did not put his fears to rest.

Instead, Mr Jennings shook his head. 'Why do you think we were all so overjoyed when you two got together? We've been waiting years for you to admit how you felt about each other.'

'But—but—' Sam had always had a soft spot for Emmy but had kept his distance out of respect for her and the family, until Dave's wedding night. His feelings for her had developed a lot more since then. He never considered hers might have too. Paris had been magical but falling in love with her had not been in his plans. That was why he had forced her hand into leaving him. He had been afraid of hurting her, the baby and himself, somewhere further down the line. These last days without her had showed him how futile that whole exercise had been when they were both hurting. Now he was finding out she might have loved him all along, he knew how much pain she was in being apart when he had been torn in two without her.

'Why is it coming as a surprise to you that she's in love with you? Surely you two talk. Why else would you have married?' It was Mrs Jennings who took a softer approach, sitting on the edge of her chair and making him think about their recent actions.

'We, uh, decided to get married for the baby's sake. A marriage of convenience to raise the baby together. Except, well, you know my family history. I didn't want to end up like my dad, never at home and oblivious to any pain I might cause. When I realised we were getting in too deep, I thought we should live different lives to avoid any misunderstanding or hurt.'

'And that's when she disappeared?'

Sam nodded, though he ought to be hanging his head in shame as he sat explaining to Mr Jennings and the others about the crazy set-up he had engineered. If they had ever thought him worthy of Emmy, that would all change after today. He could never look either of them in the eye again after this.

'David's right, you are an idiot.' Mrs Jennings verbally slapped him across the face with the insult as she stood and cleared the tea dishes away. Sam supposed it could have been worse. He certainly deserved everything they threw at him.

'Emmy's at work. Clearly, it's only you she's

avoiding.' Dave hung up before Sam had the opportunity to speak to her for himself.

'She's okay?' It was such a relief to have finally tracked her down, though he wished her colleagues might have given a heads-up and prevented him from making a show of himself here this morning.

'I told you, she's working and not very happy with me for phoning, or you for worrying everyone.'

'I'm glad you did. At least now I can tell them to call off search and rescue.' Sam attempted to rebuild some hastily destroyed bridges with some humour, now they knew everything was okay with Emmy and the baby.

'So, what are you going to do about all of this, Sam?'

'You have to go and sort things out with Emmy.'

'Stop being a moron or I'll be forced to hit you.'

Mr and Mrs Jennings, and Dave, each took a turn at trying to talk some sense into him, but Sam had already made his mind up to go and see her. It was time they were honest with each other about their feelings. Perhaps then they might actually have a chance at making things work and being a family once and for all.

'It's just a misunderstanding. Sam forgot I was staying with my parents for a few days, that's all.'

'Hmm, well, he seemed pretty concerned. You might want to give him a call.' Shelley did not look convinced by Emmy's explanation, but the state of her marriage was not gossip fodder. She wished Sam had not given people cause to question their relationship, but she supposed that was partly her fault for ignoring him this long.

In all honesty she never expected him to come looking for her when he had seemed so keen to return to his single life as soon as possible. There might also have been an element of wanting him to suffer a tiny bit, the way she had. It was backfiring on her now with her curious co-workers and her brother now involved.

'That's what happens when you're both working two different timetables. We might need to invest in a weekly planner to see what the other is doing.' She brushed off any concerns with a light laugh before resuming her duties. Until recently, lying was not something which came easily to her. Now she seemed to do it at the drop of a hat. All to cover up the fake relationship with Sam. Something which had caused no end of problems and was now redundant anyway. The only partnership they would have in the future would be in raising their child and she remained unconvinced that would even happen. Sam had proved to be as unreliable as he had always told her he was.

Now she had more trouble in store with her family if David's phone call was anything to go by. He had told her he was checking in with her after Sam had showed up on their parents' doorstep claiming she had vanished into thin air. Finding out she was still in the land of the living had satisfied him for now, but David would realise there was more going on behind the scenes than a mere tiff.

It was all such a mess, and if Sam had involved her family, she was going to have to explain the whole deal surrounding her pregnancy. Confirmation that even as an adult she was still a failure whom nobody really wanted.

Emmy rubbed her temples trying to massage away the throbbing pain lurking in her head. She had been a bit light-headed this morning and her skin was clammy in the cloying heat of the hospital. It would be no surprise if she was coming down with some sort of bug when she was so exhausted, her immune system probably too run down to fight off infection. The stress of the whole situation with Sam was something which would only continue to mar her pregnancy if she did not tackle it head-on soon. There was no more hiding. Once she was settled properly back into her flat again she would talk to Sam to sort things out as amicably as possible, but she was also going to have to tell her family everything and get it all off her chest.

Maybe then she could properly start looking forward to impending motherhood and focus her energy on the only thing that really mattered in this mess. Her baby.

'Good morning, Liam. How are you today?' Emmy set aside her own personal issues as soon as she was back on the ward.

'Good. Mum brought me some art supplies to keep me busy.' One of the tables on wheels they used at mealtimes had been commandeered as a makeshift craft table, sitting over the bed, laden with paints, paper and pencils.

'That should keep you busy. Try not to get it everywhere or you will have Sister in telling you off.' She bent down to pick up an errant scrap of paper from the floor and the dizzy sensation which overtook her almost caused Emmy to black out. It took a moment for her to regain her composure, holding on to the bedside table until everything stopped spinning.

'Are you okay, Emmy?' Liam sat up and peered over at her.

'I think I just stood up too quickly. No need to worry. I'll look forward to seeing your masterpieces later,' she reassured him before making a hasty exit.

Once out of Liam's eyeline, Emmy gave in to the need to rest against the wall outside. Her body suddenly felt as though it was on fire and she was beginning to fade out from consciousness again.

'Help.' She did not know who she was calling out to. All she could think was that something was wrong and she could be losing her baby. The chaos she and Sam had created in trying to do the right thing had been so destructive their baby was already suffering because of them.

'Emmy? What's happened? Can someone get a trolley, please?' It was Sam's voice she heard pleading for assistance, his hand which reached for hers, as she concentrated on breathing so she would not pass out.

Inhale. Exhale. Hang on, little one.

She did not know she was crying until she saw her tears making a puddle on the shiny floor.

'Stay with me, Emmy.' Sam put his arm around her shoulders and helped her remain upright until extra hands were there, urging her onto a stretcher.

'Sam? Are we losing the baby?' She was flying down the corridor at speed, the fluorescent lights above her head becoming a bright blur. All the while she could feel Sam's hand clenching hers.

'Not if we can help it. I'm so sorry for everything. I came to tell you that. No matter what happens, I am here for you. Your family are right, I am a prize idiot.'

Even in her fugue state, the odd comment managed to filter through her consciousness.

'Why would you say that? They love you.'

So do I, she said to herself as she began to drift out.

'I'll explain everything later. Just you make sure you come back to me, Emmy Goodwin. I need you. I love you.'

As blackness swirled around her, she decided her mind was playing tricks on her. Sam did not love her. Nobody did. That was why she had to keep this baby safe inside. So for the first and probably only time in her life she would have someone who loved her unconditionally. Without Sam's baby she would have nothing left to live for. She needed that ray of light to have something worth leaving this quiet darkness for and bring her back to life. Sam's voice at her ear, calling her name, was the last thing she remembered before she was lost in the abyss.

'I don't know what I'll do if anything happens to Em or the baby.' Sam was sitting in a chair in the hospital corridor, head in his hands, and feeling more powerless than he had ever felt in his life. Even when his father had gone and his mother had been at her lowest, he had been able to work and contribute something, albeit only financially. Here, now, there was literally nothing he could do to help his wife and child.

Worse than that was the knowledge that it was likely because of him their lives were in the balance.

'I hope you're not still going to try and tell me you don't love her after this.' Dave gave him a friendly pat on the back, more than Sam thought he deserved in the circumstances.

As soon as Emmy had been taken for blood tests, he had phoned the family to let them know what had happened and they had all driven down to the hospital to provide him with moral support and be closer to Emmy. If she could only see them now, faces streaked with tears, nerves shredded waiting to hear she was going to be okay, she would realise how much she was loved. Despite what she might think, she was a very much cherished member of the family and an important part of everyone's lives. Even the twins were in attendance, clearly upset that their big sister, along with their baby nephew or niece, were fighting for their lives.

His breath hitched in his throat with the reminder of what they were all going through,

Emmy in particular. He was trying to be strong for her, and the baby, but that could not stop the tears forming in his eyes. The love he had denied too long was there for everyone to see.

'Only an idiot would do that,' he said, trying to smile through the pain.

'Our Emmy won't give up without a fight,' Mr Jennings insisted, holding his wife's hand and trying to convince everyone that she would survive anything. Except she had not survived marrying Sam. It was his fault she was here, hovering between life and death.

All he had thought of was himself when he had driven her away. He had not wanted to force her into a life with him, but never stopped to think about what it was she might need. The future had seemed so scary to him, under pressure to be a good husband and father, but those were the roles he had accepted, and he should have done better. If he had not been so wrapped up in his own feelings, he might have seen what the rest of the family could. That they loved each other, and both were afraid to admit to it. One open, honest conversation, instead of dodging around their fears about the consequences, could have prevented all of this.

It was understandable that she hadn't confided in him, if everything her family said was true, when emotional attachment was not something he had encouraged. Looking back, it made sense about why she had agreed to marry him in the first place. Emmy was a romantic; she would never have dreamed of going through with a wedding simply because it was the logical thing to do. Everything she did was filled with love and commitment, although he had apparently been blind to it until now when it could be too late to do something about it.

Sam did not regret marrying Emmy or getting her pregnant, and he should never have let her think that he did. The upset and stress so early in the pregnancy was not good for her or the baby but he had neglected to consider any of that. He did not even know where she had been living since moving out when it clearly was not with her family. Who knew what conditions she had had to put up with in the interim because she had been too embarrassed by the situation he had put her in to go to her parents?

'Emmy is also more fragile than any of us realise. We are all guilty of ignoring her feelings because it's more convenient. Without meaning to upset anyone more, she has been suffering for a long time. I totally hold my hands up and say I'm the most recent cause of her heartache and take full responsibility for that. As soon as she is through this, I am going to be the best husband and father I can be.' His voice broke, his very soul calling out for her to be well enough to give him a chance to prove his sincerity on that score.

'What do you mean she's been suffering for a long time? Did you know she was ill?' Mrs Jennings's hand was on her heart, that same pain Sam was feeling obviously causing her distress too.

'I mean emotionally. Emmy is very sensitive and sometimes, well, she doesn't feel as though she fits in, or at least that she isn't wanted.' He looked pointedly at the twins, who had the decency to hang their heads.

Mrs Jennings gasped but it was Mr Jennings who strongly refuted Sam's comment. 'Emmy was always wanted. She is very much part of the family.'

'Sam's right, Dad. We don't always stick up

for her when these two can't keep their snide remarks to themselves. The rest of us don't take it personally but for Emmy I guess there is always going to be an issue about being a real member of the family.' Dave jumped in to echo Sam's thoughts, and though he was grateful for the backup, he wished they weren't having this conversation at all.

'We don't mean anything by it.'

'We'll never do it again. I promise we'll try to do better.'

The twins sniffed and genuinely looked upset enough Sam wanted to believe them.

'We might not be blood, but Emmy is our daughter, and nothing is going to change that. I had no idea she felt that way, but we are all going to do better for her.' A determined-sounding Mrs Jennings spoke for the whole of the family, with all nodding their heads in agreement. As a group of people who were supposed to love Emmy enough for her to feel secure, Sam included, they had failed her. He could only hope along with everyone else that they got to make amends and could look forward to welcoming the next generation of the family.

CHAPTER TWELVE

EMMY TRIED TO lick her lips, they were so dry, but even that seemed a task too far in her current state. She was hovering in the dark somewhere between sleep and consciousness, trying to find her way back to the light.

'Emmy? Are you awake? I think she's trying to come to. I can see her eyes moving.' A familiar voice was out there somewhere. One she really wanted to hear.

'Sam?' Her voice was little more than a croak, but it seemed to get his attention as she felt a hand grip onto hers.

'I'm here, Emmy. Open your eyes and you'll see.' Regardless of everything that had passed between them, Sam was here, and she wanted to see him again. It had been too long without him.

There were other voices and sounds going on around her, but she blocked them out to focus on the one she wanted to hear most in that moment. With every ounce of strength she could muster she forced her eyes to open. It took a few seconds for her to focus, everything seemed so bright.

'Sam?' she said again, searching for him.

He squeezed her hand. 'I'm right here by your bed.'

Emmy turned her head a fraction and watched as his handsome face came into view. 'You haven't shaved,' she noted, trying to lift her hand to stroke the dark stubble lining his taut jaw.

He smiled and rubbed her fingers across the bristles. 'I've been a bit preoccupied worrying about you.'

'Me?' She was delving into her brain trying to remember what had happened and where she was. Everything was so jumbled, and nothing made sense. Why was she in bed feeling so rough and why was Sam here after they had split up?

It all came rushing back to her in one overwhelming wave of emotion. Sam's harsh words…leaving their home…working…then the blackness… She dropped his hand and placed hers on her stomach. The tears came even though she was too tired to cry.

'The baby… I'm so sorry.' For her, him and the child who would never get to take its first breath. She should have reached out and asked someone to help instead of trying to do everything herself. It was her fear of not fitting in, of having to admit she had failed, which had cost their baby its life. Her fault.

'Shh.' Sam brushed away her tears and kissed her gently on the cheek. His soft touch, so loving and gentle, only made her cry for what they could have had together if things had been different. 'Everything's going to be okay. Our little one is every bit as stubborn and strong as its mother.'

Still woozy, his words did not register straight away. Then she saw the grin on his face. 'You mean—?'

'Our baby is hanging in there. An infection led to maternal sepsis. That's what caused you to pass out. You were running a high temperature, and you gave us quite a scare, but they gave you fluids and antibiotics. As long as you take care from now on, hopefully there won't be any more drama for the rest of the pregnancy.'

'Hey, honey. We're so glad you're both doing okay.' It was then she noticed her father in the room and her heart swelled a bit more. He walked over and gave her a peck on the cheek, followed by her weeping mother.

'I'm so sorry, Emmy, if we ever made you feel left out. We just took it for granted you knew how much we loved you. You're our daughter, no matter what biology says.'

Emmy managed to sit up and give her mother a half-hug because she looked as though she needed it. Just as she was dealing with her parents' unusual display of emotion, Lorna and Lisa rallied on both sides of the bed to hug her in tandem.

'We are so sorry for every mean thing we ever did or said to you.'

'Can you ever forgive us? We will be the best aunties ever. Promise.'

Emmy glanced at Sam, who did not fool her with his attempt to look innocent. She was sure it was not only the life or death experience which had prompted this sudden outburst from her family; he had a hand in this somewhere and she was grateful.

Even David was there with a kiss and hug, apparently too choked to say more than 'It's good to have you back, sis.'

'Do you think Emmy and I could have a

moment in private together?' Sam asked the others. Emmy wondered how they had all managed to get in here with visitors usually limited to one or two. Again, something Sam had probably arranged but she could not figure out why he would have gone to so much trouble, when he had made it clear he did not want her the last time they had seen each other.

'Sure. Let's go, folks, and let these two sort things out.' Her father herded the others out of the hospital side room, his words indicating she had missed a lot while asleep.

'Sam? What's going on? I mean, I'm grateful you are all here but if I'm okay there is no need for you to stick around. Don't feel as though you have to pretend any more. We agreed to the split.' Even though that particular memory was breaking her heart all over again.

'I'm done pretending, Emmy. I'm here with you because I want to be.'

'What does that mean, Sam? I'm too tired to keep guessing what it is you really want.' Her head was still fuzzy; bits and pieces of memories, or dreams, were slowly coming back to her and she was trying to decipher which were real or in her mind. Like hearing him tell her he loved her.

That had to be her mind playing tricks on her, letting her believe she had something worth living for before she had lost consciousness. Sam had made it clear to her that the honeymoon was over and, with it, his desire to be a real husband to her. She had been getting ready to start her life over again, learning to live without him, when disaster had struck. Now the danger had passed, she did not want to take two steps back, with Sam thinking he had to take responsibility for her. They had been there, done that, and it had not worked out first time around. Next time she settled down it would be with someone who loved her as much as she loved him. She and the baby deserved nothing less.

'I want you to come home with me.'

Emmy sighed. As much as she wanted that, she had learned not to accept Sam into her life at any cost. It hurt too much. She could not afford to be selfish any more if it meant putting her baby at risk again as well as her heart.

'Sam… I'm not a problem you have to keep fixing. We tried to do the right thing, but it didn't work out. You have no reason to feel guilty or as though you're obligated to take me back simply because I ended up in here. I'm fine. I've got my old flat back for now, and if it comes to it, I'll transfer out near my folks.'

'Why would you do that when you have a job here, a home with me to come back to and our baby on the way?'

It sounded so straightforward put like that, but the reality had been somewhat different. Emmy knew dreams did not always work out exactly the way she wanted. She was married to Sam and expecting his baby but that was where the fantasy ended because he did not love her. This was her wake-up call, as well as closure on her marriage.

'Sam… I know I said I could co-habit and co-parent with you, that marriage would be in name only, no strings attached. The truth is…' She gulped in a deep breath. 'The truth is I have feelings for you and that compli-cates things.'

'What sort of feelings?'

'Pardon me?'

'I can understand if it's disappointment you feel towards me, maybe even a very strong dislike, after the way I behaved. If it's something more than that, I would like to know.'

'Why? So I can be humiliated even more? Why does it matter now? It doesn't make any difference to our situation.' Except to put more pressure on him to do the 'right thing' when it was not necessary. Emmy had her family and soon she would have her baby. There would be plenty of love in her life.

'Because I don't want to be the one to say, "I love you," and not hear it back.' Sam looked at her sheepishly, reminding her of the teen who used to visit her brother but probably spent more time with her. Could it really be true that he loved her? Her heart gave an optimistic extra beat which registered on the monitor by the bed.

'Do you mean it? I don't want you to say it simply to get me to agree to go home with you and salve your conscience.'

Sam shook his head. 'I was coming to tell you before you took ill. I've been going out of my mind without you. I'm sorry I drove you away. With everything that went on with my dad, I was afraid of repeating history. That's no excuse, I know. I hurt you and that was the one thing I was trying not to do. By admitting that I had fallen for you, I thought it would only make things harder. I didn't want to fail you but that's exactly what I've done.'

'You haven't failed anyone. Although I'm still waiting for those three little words…' Emmy would not believe this was happening until she heard them and could be confident she was not having some sort of pain-induced hallucination.

Sam cupped her face in his hands and leaned in, so he was only a breath away. 'I love you, Emmy. I probably always have, though I was too stupid to realise it. I'm here for you, if you want me?'

They were the words that Emmy always wanted to hear but for her sake and the baby's she had to be sure there was something more behind them to ensure a different outcome if she went back to Sam.

'I love you too but is that enough, Sam? It wasn't before.' This might all be new to him but to her it was familiar ground. She loved him but he had practically thrown her out of the house, told her he did not want a 'real' marriage. What had changed over these past few days other than him realising he missed her?

'I wasn't being honest with you or myself because I was afraid of the consequences. All I can offer you now is my love and a promise I will do better by you in the future.'

He pushed his chair back and got down on one knee by the bed. 'I love you, Mrs Goodwin, and hope that you will do me the honour of becoming my wife again.'

Emmy smiled through her happy tears. He got extra points for the proposal this time. 'Yes. Yes, I will, Mr Goodwin.'

If Sam was facing his fears and going all in with the relationship, desperately trying to exorcise the ghosts of his past, Emmy too needed to leave her insecurities behind in the name of love. Sam had been a constant in her life for a very long time, loving her for exactly who she was. It had simply taken them this long to realise it.

EPILOGUE

Fifteen months later

'YOU MAY NOW kiss the bride.'

Emmy grinned at her husband, waiting for him to repeat that passionate kiss along with their wedding vows. Instead, Sam reached for the baby, who she had been holding throughout the ceremony.

'I think Abigail would like to spend some time with her adoring aunties.' He passed their daughter to Lorna and Lisa to fuss over her.

Despite their history, Emmy had asked them to be godparents to the baby. She wanted them to be part of her family, and since the scare early on in her pregnancy, they had been nothing but kind to Emmy. They had turned out to be amazing aunts who absolutely doted on their little niece. The whole family did.

Once Emmy's arms were free, Sam wrapped his around her and gave her a kiss to rival the leading man in any romantic movie. They were more in love now than ever and making up for lost time. Even with a young baby to look after, they made time for each other. Their relationship took priority over everything and Emmy could not have been happier.

Today was a double celebration. Abigail's christening followed by a renewal of their wedding vows. Something they both wanted to do over, so they got it right this time. Marrying for love and being honest about it.

Sam was a wonderful husband, as well as being a hands-on dad, and had finally put to rest his fears about becoming a carbon copy of his own father.

'I have a surprise for you, Mrs Goodwin,' he said, whispering into her ear.

'Another one?' Emmy had to be the luckiest woman in the world when he was constantly showing her how much he loved her with thoughtful gifts and sweet gestures, in case she ever forgot.

'Your parents have agreed to babysit so we can go on honeymoon.'

'Where?' Emmy gasped. As much as she

loved her baby and would miss her, the thought of a few days alone with Sam sounded like heaven.

'Where else? Paris.' He grinned at her, knowing he deserved a gold star for pulling this one out of the bag.

Emmy let out a squeal before hugging him tightly. 'I love you, Sam Goodwin.'

'Good. This marriage lark is supposed to work out better when both parties can admit that. I love you too, Emmy Goodwin.'

Emmy's husband kissed her long and hard, and she did not care who was watching. After all, they were among family.

* * * * *

If you enjoyed this story, check out these other great reads from Karin Baine

The Nurse's Christmas Hero
The Surgeon and the Princess
One Night with Her Italian Doc
Reunion with His Surgeon Princess

All available now!